INFERNAL JUSTICE

MEN OF VANGUARD BOOK 2

RYDER O'MALLEY

MEN OF VANGUARD SERIES

MEN OF VANGUARD

Infamous Heart

Infernal Justice

Iridescent Light

1

COFFEE. IF THERE WASN'T A CUP ON THE TABLE IN THREE seconds, today would be the day I destroy mankind. Let the countdown to supervillainy begin. One. Twenty-four hours of ensuring the city's heroes didn't die had taken its toll. Two. Our so-called saviors were no help as they destroyed everything in their path. Three—

"One cup of liquid death for you." Griffin set the cup on the table. "And it looks like it couldn't come soon enough."

To this day, I have no idea why we started coming to the HideOut as part of our morning ritual. The coffee shop served as a hub for the community. While not exclusively gay clientele, the owner, Chad, and his husband didn't hide their relationship, and other gay men took notice. Now you couldn't throw an espresso cup without hitting a gay hipster on a coffee date.

Alejandro bit into his avocado toast, but that didn't prevent him from speaking. "He did that thing again."

"What thing?" I asked, knowing full well I wouldn't like the answer. Three sets of eyes fixated on me.

Bernard leaned forward, placing one of his massive paws over my hand. "Xander, were you plotting the destruction of mankind again?"

"No." The coffee burned, almost stinging my tongue, but I didn't care. After a night of keeping patients from crossing the threshold to death, it had worn me raw. It would probably have been smart to skip breakfast with the guys and head home, but they'd all agree—sometimes I'm too stubborn for my own good.

"Definitely destruction of the world," Alejandro said as he shoved the last bite into his mouth. "Is there a coffee equivalent to being hangry? Congry?"

As usual, Alejandro rambled, no longer taking part in the actual conversation. He could be flighty, but he was also one of the funniest people I had ever met. Give him a minute and he'll come back to the conversation with something outlandish that would cause everybody to pause and chuckle.

Bernard, on the other hand, didn't have a humorous bone in his body. The man woke up serious, as if the guilt of the world rested solely on his shoulders. It was part of why we never made it to a second date. It also didn't help that when it came time for one of us to mount the other, we realized that tops make terrible bottoms. Thankfully, a night of awkward sex didn't diminish a long-standing friendship.

"Rough night?" Griffin asked.

And then there was Griffin, the newest acquisition to the group. Geek extraordinaire, and overly nice guy. Everybody at the table would agree that I had a bit of a temper issue. I liked to think of Griffin as the counter to that. He was generally mellow, and the only things that ever got him excited were art and comics. Oh, and supers.

"The Doctors of Disaster struck the financial district." There was no way to hide rolling my eyes, so I let those whites shine brightly. "Third-tier villains who somehow scored a shipment of vaporizing tech from the B'Nethian aliens. It was chaos."

"Huffee," Alejandro blurted out. "He's huffee."

Bernard spat his coffee into his cup. Griffin's lips curled as he fought off a laugh. Even as I shot daggers at each of them, they burst out laughing. Okay, I had to admit, maybe, once in a great while, I got "huffee." It came with seeing the worst mankind had to offer. This was the reason I came to breakfast with these three every morning. They served as a reset, a reminder that not all of the universe burned in a horrible train wreck.

"As you were saying." Bernard hid his smirk with a cup of coffee.

"It started at the banks. At that hour they're closed and

only have electronic security, no big deal for me. But then they moved on to some research labs on the east side. There were night crews working and things got messy."

"Who saved the day?"

I admired Griffin's naïveté, no lie. He truly believed that superheroes flew in, saved the day, and the world went back to normal. It wasn't just him. Most of the normal people thought the heroes were these godlike saviors. No, for those of us on the front lines dealing with the fallout, we knew the truth. Superheroes were just as bad as the villains they fought.

"You mean, which superhero used his flame abilities and left a man with second-degree burns? Or which set of laser eyes caused a floor to collapse, trapping three inside?"

Griffin leaned back in his chair, painfully aware he had struck a nerve. I didn't *hate* superheroes, though he might argue that fact with how I spoke about them. I hated that they came in, beat up a bad guy, took a few photos, offered a few quotes for the magazines, and then left. Behind them, death, destruction, and paramedics like me see to the victims after each battle.

I ground my teeth at the thought. I *should* see to the victims, but as part of the Supers Emergency Medical Services, the only patients I could treat were the supposed heroes who saved the day. Bitter? Who me?

"Sorry, apparently I'm *huffee*."

"I don't want to harp on your personal hygiene."

Alejandro grabbed one of my hands, holding my fingers upright. "But what have we told you about blood at the breakfast table?"

Normally I'd wait till I got home to scrub away the filth, but a rebar spike had impaled Heron. His wings or forearm blades were no match for hemorrhaging and blood loss. This is where my team came in. The Hero Brigade. Somebody in the government thought the lives of heroes were more important than that burn victim or the people under the rubble. Instead of saving average humans, I was tasked with saving people with abilities.

"Like I said, it was a long night." I stared at the red under my nails. I didn't need to check the HeroApp™ to know there was a big black shield next to Heron's name. He hadn't survived the ride to the hospital.

"Topic switch." No medic enjoyed talking about a call where they lost the patient. "So, Griffin, getting railed regularly?"

Alejandro's eyes lit up. Leave it to our resident sexpert to jump at the opportunity. "Is Sebastian a post-sex cuddle covered in cum kind of guy, or does he instantly need a shower?"

Now it was Griffin giving me a death glare. Nothing swapped topics faster than bad dates and horrible sex. But when those weren't available, talking about Griffin's hunky boyfriend was a good filler.

"I hate you," he mouthed.

"If he's doing it right, there shouldn't be a mess." I nearly choked on my coffee as Bernard offered his personal insight. He had a knack for injecting his dry wit at the best of times. I eyed the bearish man. I might need to revisit my aversion to taking cock.

Alejandro held up a finger at Bernard. "We're going to revisit your etiquette in the bedroom, you nasty bear. First, Griffin, we're dying to hear."

Out of nowhere, Chad stood at the table, pouring a cup of coffee setting it in front of the man. "Leave him alone. We already know he's a shower in the morning kind of guy. Xander, how about you tell us about that fling you were parading around last week?"

Griffin gave the barista a high-five. Well played Chad, well played. He was the unofficial fifth member of the breakfast club. His ability to appear whenever a cup ran dry or when the conversation turned toward dating and sex bordered on supernatural.

"He's ancient history." Truth be told, he had texted asking if I wanted to get together again. He was a sweet guy, which in my world spelled disaster. Sweet men weren't the type to put up with my collection of baggage.

Alejandro raised an eyebrow. "You know you can go on a second date with a guy and not get married, right? It might do you some good to have somebody to come home to."

Great, I was getting dating advice from a man who

struggled to remember the name of the last superhero he rode like a nickel steed outside of the drugstore. "Okay, I think we've had enough discussion about my love life."

Alejandro turned to Griffin and continued grilling him about his new boyfriend. Bernard, however, leaned onto the table. His twitching mustache gave away the impending sagely advice. Out of this crew, he balanced out our overly emotional responses with a calm demeanor.

His eyes softened as he reached under the table, resting his hand on my thigh. He gave it a firm squeeze. "I think a second date is exactly what you need."

That was easier said than done.

2

"I'M NOT GOING TO WATCH THEM DIE."

Lei grabbed my arm. Her brow wrinkled as she prepared to deliver a sarcastic comment for violating the administration's rule book. She proved herself to be a superb partner in the truck, and I couldn't think of many medics I'd rather have at my six. But when it came to the primary people we were directed to help, she listened to the bigwigs. I, on the other hand, cared more about saving lives.

"If they write you up again—"

"The goddamned bridge is collapsing. There are people out there." I knew she was waiting to save a fallen hero, but how could she ignore their panicked screams? While Lei could sit in the ambulance and watch innocents plunge to their deaths, my training took hold.

I shoved the passenger door open and jumped out. We had arrived on-site to provide medical attention to Dr. Arcane and his mystics. A portal on the far side of the bridge had opened and out poured a small army of golems. These magical creatures had been created by some evil villain, but it was up to the Doc and his sidekicks to stop them. Nowhere in the expectations did it say, "Do not destroy the bridge into Vanguard City."

I followed the massive cable on the side of the bridge until I discovered the problem. The thinner wires connecting the bridge to the suspension cable had severed, torn away, and now more threatened to break. With a volley of fireballs, the heroes annihilated the front row of the muddy beasts, but the explosions rocked the bridge enough that a chasm formed.

While they prepared their next spells, the crack widened, cars falling into the river below. People leapt from their vehicles, running away from the growing hole in the middle of the bridge. It would only be a matter of minutes before the center of the bridge collapsed.

"Help." The meek voice barely rose above the bolts of pink lightning thrown by Dr. Arcane. Jogging toward the hole, a cubbish man caught me by the arm.

"Leave it to the heroes." His glasses were bent, nearly obscuring the cut above his right eye. "The bridge is collapsing." He was a thick man. Dare I say chubby? If he hadn't tried to prevent me from doing my job, I might have offered to buy him a coffee.

I yanked my arm away. "I know, asshole."

Picking up the pace, I reached the edge of the expanding hole. Asphalt continued breaking away, toppling hundreds of feet into the icy river below. Dr. Arcane should have turned his attention to the civilians, the people unable to protect themselves. Instead, he showed off for the public, giving his ego a sloppy hand job.

"Help!"

A dark blue car jerked as the road under the rear wheel crumbled. The door had been dented, hit with enough force it trapped the driver inside. No thinking, just acting. I ran, grabbed the door handle, and lifted with all my might. Even the frequent trips to the gym hadn't given me enough strength to tear the door from its frame.

"Don't leave me." His eyes were desperate, pleading with me not to abandon him. Reaching for the pocket on my thigh, I fished around for the cold metal.

"Turn your face away." He listened without question. Gripping the utility tool, I smash it against the window. "Can you climb out?"

"My seatbelt—" I don't need to hear the end of his statement. I smashed the glass, clearing enough for me to lean through the window.

"Thank you." He's terrified, his voice trembling like a man about to die. I flipped the tool around, snaking it between his waist and the seatbelt. It took a few jerks, but I tore through the fabric.

"Climb," I barked.

He pulled himself through the window, trying to avoid the remaining glass. The moment I could get my arms under his armpits, I carried his weight, dragging him free of the car. As soon as he hit the asphalt, he was crawling, scurrying to his feet and bolting away from the car.

His car groaned as the asphalt gave way. I tried to jump, but it was too late. I was going down. My fingers slid along the road, trying to find anything to slow my descent. Just before I plummeted downward, my fingers dug into a crack in the pavement. Hanging hundreds of feet above the river, I tried to count my blessings.

The hole continued to expand, and it was only a matter of time before I fell through the air. I was only a few feet from reaching the surface of the street, but it might as well have been a mile away. Swinging my weight, I grabbed onto a piece of rebar. No matter how hard I swung my leg up, I couldn't pull myself any higher. Hanging, minutes from death, I should have assumed that it'd be a superhero that did me in. I'd curse Dr. Arcane as I plummeted into the water below.

All that time spent at the gym, building muscle to back my mouth, none of it could have prepared me for this. Switching my weight to my other hand, the fatigue set in.

Already, my body grew heavy, and I struggled to maintain my grip.

A hand shot over the ledge, fingers digging into my wrist. I was glad to see there was another person out here with a moral compass pointing North. Another hand joined the first, grabbing me by the back of my uniform, pulling me upward. It wasn't a graceful rescue, but it was enough that I could get my leg onto the pavement and roll away from the hole. From now on, I'd do pull-ups at the gym.

The road continued to break apart, but for a second, I was safe. My savior fell back on his butt, gasping for air. When I looked up, it surprised me to see the man from earlier, the asshole who warned me away.

"Surprised?" he asked between gasps.

"Yeah, I am." I got to my knees, scrambling to get away from the hole as the ground lurched.

"You looked like you were having *so* much fun."

"Great, a comedian." I got to my feet, holding out a hand. With a grunt, I pulled the large man to his feet. Inches from my face, he didn't hide his smirk. Great, he knew I owed him my life, and I had a feeling he'd make good on that debt.

"Aren't you supposed to be the one saving lives?" I debated jumping through the hole. Death couldn't be more grating than his attempts at humor.

"The witty banter is best left to Dr. Arcane and his henchmen."

"You didn't see? They had to fall back. It's an all-alert invasion now. There are heroes out here I've never even heard of." This would have been like Christmas for Griffin. He was constantly asking about the heroes I got called to save.

"We need to get out of here." Scanning the bridge, I couldn't see any more civilians. Had they all gotten away? Had the new wave of supers saved them? It was the two of us that needed to get to safety before we became another superpowered casualty.

I jerked away when he tried to grab my wrist. His head tilted to the side, offended I didn't let some stranger grab at me. The big guy might be cute, but not so much that I wouldn't lay him out flat.

A cable snapped, flying overhead before the bridge shifted. "Run!" He was already bolting into a sprint when I finished the command. I was many things, but fast was not one of them. Before we had gone a hundred feet, I daydreamed that I had let go of the rebar and plummeted to my death. I wouldn't even run toward cake.

"What's that?" He slowed to a saunter, pointing toward the divider that split the lanes on the bridge. I had a moment to inspect the sky. The golems weren't the problem anymore. Harpies soaring through the air had taken priority. The fight had started with Dr. Arcane's magicians, but it had grown in scope and there must have been a hundred heroes shooting lasers, summoning lightning, or hammering flying demons with their fists.

"Medic, give me a hand."

I stumbled forward as a harpy shot upward, striking a winged hero. The two barreled toward the bridge, trading blows with neither getting the upper hand. In the middle of the carnage, it was impossible to tell if the good guys were winning. Having destroyed the bridge into the city, no matter who won, the normal folk were losing.

The man didn't slow despite the chaos, moving toward the side of the bridge where piles of cars had been flipped. I was about to yell for him to keep running toward safety when he barked, "There's somebody alive!"

I had been a medic for years, and as long as somebody still had a bit of fight left, it was my job to make sure they didn't die before we reached the hospital. Then it was up to the doctors to fix the problem.

"I don't recognize him."

A man with a jetpack flew overhead, grabbing a harpy by the wings as I slowed my pace. I reached the man, and true to his word, a green man—no, alien, was lying on the ground, one of his four arms stretched out. I didn't have my emergency bag, so I'd have to do this old school.

"Is he one of the good guys?"

I ignored the question. It wasn't my place to assign good or bad. It was inconsequential to my job. I pushed aside my personal feelings as I dropped to my knees next to the alien. They weren't as common as terrestrial heroes, but I had treated my fair share in the back of the ambulance.

"You need to run," I barked.

"I'm not leaving—"

"No," I growled, "I need you to tell my partner I need her. She's waiting a ways up the bridge. Big white box truck. Go. Now!"

He hesitated, eyeing me. I appreciated he was willing to stay in the middle of a shit show to see this through. When the apocalypse stopped, I'd be sure to find him. I owed him my life.

"Aiden," he said, "Aiden Scott."

"Thank you."

With a salute, he turned and bolted. I had to admire his ass. It looked rather tasty as he dashed off.

I rested a hand on the alien's neck. His pulse was bounding, thumping from a familiar two-heart gallop.

"Okay, so far, not a corpse."

The hero's eyes were almost serpentine, yellow, and narrow. I pulled a penlight from my pocket. With a click, I checked his eyes. One pupil blown, no iris to be found. Dammit, if he's herniating, I'd be carrying a corpse to the truck.

Explosions.

I dropped onto all fours, covering the alien as a car launched upward. The heat washed over my body as debris skid along the street. I imagined dying in the line of duty, but it wasn't going to be today, not because a bunch of second-rate heroes couldn't stop a simple alien invasion.

The harpies were scary, but I'd gladly punch the winged hell beasts. However, in the middle of the road, a shadowy figure stood watching. Its lengthy arms hung below its knees, black fingers dragging along the pavement. It'd be ominous on its own, but as its body jerked as if staving off a seizure, I fought to control my bladder. Staring in my direction, I swore the beast grinned.

"Goddammit," I growled, "we're screwed."

3

THE SHADOW DIDN'T RUN SO MUCH AS STALK FORWARD. ITS arms went out wide, preparing to lunge if I ran. I couldn't outrun molasses, let alone a supernatural creature. The alien grabbed onto my wrist, and I stole a glance at the agony written across his face.

"Don't die on me now."

Other than an extra set of appendages, he didn't appear to have any weapons. Scouring the ground for a weapon, I reached for a tire iron. It wasn't nearly as impressive as the ten smoky blades attached to the shadow's hands, but it would have to do.

"I'll be right back." Maybe.

My fingers tightened on the piece of metal. If I could get close enough, perhaps duck under its hands and strike upward, I could impale the creature. Leaning forward, I charged, preparing to stop short, hopefully out of reach of its hands. A simple fake and misdirect, the thing couldn't be that smart. Evil shadow monsters were dumb, right?

As I stopped short, hoping I gauged its striking distance correctly, it surprised me with a swift turn. With one arm stretched out, it batted at me, and into the air I sailed. Smacking asphalt, I rolled to my knees, praying it didn't take up the chase.

Instead, the thing laughed.

It stopped when the back end of the ambulance slammed into it. The crumpled body fell underneath a tire as Lei spun the wheel. It'd have been a high-five moment, but she ruined it when she slammed the brakes and backed up to drive over it again. She smiled through the passenger window, two thumbs raised high. That smart ass probably waited until she could save the day.

I patted down my body, searching for anything poking in the wrong direction. Bruised ribs, maybe cracked, but otherwise I'd survive. Our patient might not be so lucky if we didn't get him out of the war zone and into a hospital.

"Man down," I yelled.

Lei jumped from the driver's seat and, in a well-rehearsed manner, had the gurney out of the back. We didn't have time to secure the patient. Based on the bruising, he had internal bleeding. We skipped the collar. Lei raised the side of his body and I slid the board under his back. We'd strap him in once we drove away, for now we lifted, putting him on the gurney.

"I've never seen him before," Lei said.

"Me either."

"Check the blood for acid." I appreciated the advice. Last time it had eaten through my pants and left a nasty scar on my thigh.

We wheeled him to the ambulance, sliding him inside. I jumped in the back and seconds later, Lei had us flying toward the hospital. I had the alligator clip on his finger as I grabbed the cuff for blood pressure. Supers with multiple limbs always posed a challenge, so it was down to picking the easiest arm to check his blood pressure.

The monitor went to work, spitting out numbers. Hypoxic. That would explain the incoherent mumbles from the hero. The constant starts and stops didn't hinder me as I grabbed a needle and started an IV. The moment I hit a vein, I grabbed the tape from the bar, securing the line. Did he have a heart? Or multiple hearts? Sometimes I longed to work on humans and their predictable organ placement.

I grabbed the scissors and pulled at the suit around his neck. When I couldn't pull it away from his body, I let out a low growl. There were plenty of heroes with suits biologically attached to their bodies. It served as protection of their secret identity, but it made my life difficult. I hated difficult. As I applied the leads to his body, I hoped I could get a reading.

"Dammit," I mumbled.

The numbers didn't indicate Cushing's triad. It meant the alien's physiology didn't align with my equipment. Unlike other trucks, we had tech onboard supplied from the heroes themselves. I reached for the cubby with the Machinist's nanobots. I hated relying on their tech, but when conventional methods failed—

"It is time." I nearly jumped at the sound of the alien's voice. The deep bass almost sounded musical.

"Time for what?" It was a stupid question. I already knew the answer. The patient verbally acknowledged that he was ready to die. We only had minutes until we reached the hospital. As long as he was talking, he wasn't dead, and everybody knew heroes liked a good monologue. Simple superhero logic.

"There is a darkness coming," he muttered.

His hand reached out, all six fingers extended in my direction. For all the tools at my disposal, none of them could diagnose the problem. Alien physiology be damned. I wasn't in the mood to lose another patient.

I grabbed his hand. His fingers wrapped about my knuckles, stronger than should be logical. He pulled me in close, his thin lips moving but not making a sound.

He finally spoke in a whisper. "It is you."

"Me?" Delirium set in. Everything out of his mouth

from this point on would be the result of his brain coping with his impending death.

"I can protect you from the darkness."

His eyes narrowed, intensifying as he pulled my hand to his chest. The EKG slowed, his heart rate dropping. I tried to pull free, to get to the equipment, but he held fast. I tugged again, but his grip was absolute. At any second, I knew he was going to box.

"It comes."

The suit under my hand separated, pulling away like oil and water. His skin underneath was covered in scars, an almost tribal pattern similar to Pe'a tattoos. They flared, burning away his suit until his entire body glowed.

"You okay back there?" Lei asked while swerving around the corner. "Xander? Man, you okay?"

All that remained of the alien's suit was a spot of black the size of a quarter. It moved down the center of his chest until it touched my thumb. I pulled with all my might, nearly tearing him off the stretcher. The black spot vanished underneath my hand. Whatever he was doing, I wanted no part of it.

"It protects the worthy."

The monitor stopped beeping. One continuous tone meant the alien's hearts had stopped. His eyes shut, the muscles in his body relaxing. I pulled myself free, prepared to bring him back from the dead. There was no way I was repeating my last shift. He was going to make—

The black started at my fingertips. The veins along my hand and arm bulged, thick and black. Had he infected me? Was I about to fall victim to the same fate? I scratched at my hand as the black oozed outward, coating my skin. Expanding, it shot up my arm, vanishing under my sleeve. I couldn't feel it moving, but seconds later my other hand was colored a flat black.

"What the hell?" The reflection in the storage door looked like me, but not. It had already coated my entire body.

"Holy shit," Lei yelled.

I turned to see her leaning over the steering wheel staring up into the sky. Before I could ask what was going on, a blinding flash of light shot through the front window. As quickly as it appeared, the world returned to normal.

The ambulance jerked to one side as she spun the wheel. I caught my reflection—the black alien ooze gone. Had I imagined it? Lack of sleep had played tricks on medics, but I swore the alien had done something. Staring at the body on the table, he was now naked, his scars no longer shining.

The truck slowed until Lei put it in park. She rushed into the back, but there was no hurry. For the second time in two days, I had lost a hero before we reached the hospital. I slumped back in the seat, staring at the alien's unmoving chest, the monitor continuing to taunt me.

I had failed.

4

I HAD BEEN TOLD TO TAKE THE REST OF THE DAY TO GET MY head together. In the middle of a superpowered emergency, I must look pretty bad to be relieved of duty. I should have gone home, stood under a scalding shower and called it a night. There were plenty of things I should do, but I remained fixated on watching the paramedics bring in a steady stream of patients.

They had picked up another hero. After twenty, I stopped keeping count. It was going to be a long night inside the walls of every hospital in Vanguard City. Government vans had arrived. Even the Centurions' science team showed their nerdy faces. In all my years, I had never seen so many humans rushing to save the heroes who were supposed to protect them.

"Ironic, isn't it?" Aiden, formerly known as the asshole, said.

"What's that?" My voice sounded unamused and lackluster to even me.

"They're the heroes. They can fly and hurl fireballs, but now it's up to good ol' science to save the day. Everyday folks have to become the heroes."

"Yeah, I guess."

His hands were wedged in his jacket pockets, so he used his foot to tap my shin. "I'm trying to pay you a compliment."

"He died."

Death and I were strange bedfellows. I rarely dwelt on losing a patient. I couldn't without going crazy. Instead, I'd run through my procedures to see if there was anything I could do differently. Eventually my case would be up for review, and I'd sit across from our medical director and be told what I could have done faster, better.

"I'm sorry."

Those not in the profession never knew how to console us on an off day. It wasn't a missing stapler or forgetting to include fries. Our bad days meant people died.

"What are you doing here?"

I looked up to see his face studying the influx of people arriving at the hospital. He was hunting for somebody in particular. Eye-level with his belt buckle, I couldn't help but let my eyes travel downward. Any other day, I'd have let out a whistle at the bulge in his jeans.

"I was at the bridge and this random dude nearly fell to his death." I looked up from his package to see him grinning. Caught. "I thought I'd stop by and see if he was going to pull through."

Smooth, I'd give him that. "Nice try. Why are you *really* here?"

"Okay, but your biceps are a perk." Was he flirting? Where the hell was Alejandro when I needed him? "Did you see the light?"

"Yeah, Lei nearly crashed the ambulance. Never seen anything like that in Vanguard. And I mean..." I gestured to a seven-foot cyborg stomping its way into the emergency room.

"Not just Vanguard. There are reports from around the globe. My boss asked me to see if I could get an official statement from one of the heroes."

"A reporter?"

"Well, sort of. I work on the blog for Revelations. A reporter hopeful, you could say. If all goes well, this story could get me bumped up to the big leagues."

I was about to ask if he knew Griffin or his boyfriend when somebody caught his attention. He put a hand on my shoulder and quickly retracted it.

"Boundaries," —he tapped a finger on his temple— "see, I can learn. Hate to jet, but I need to keep my job."

"Always grinding," I said.

"If you're lucky." Okay, screw Alejandro, even I could read the signs. My eyes must have gone wide as he laughed to himself. And with that, Aiden rushed off in pursuit of his story.

I watched his ass as he jogged toward the automatic doors. It was a bad day, but I wasn't dead. I always enjoyed a man with extra padding. It made for a cushion when things got *vigorous* in the bedroom. Before I knew it, I imagined the guy who saved my life naked.

"Shit," I cursed. I forgot to thank him for saving me. If this funk continued much longer, I was going to crawl into my cave and never leave. I might not be the most approachable person, but Mom raised me to have manners.

"Good luck, kid," I muttered. At least somebody still had the chance for their day to be better than mine.

5

"Oomph."

The chain attached to the bag jingled as I landed a right hook. Before it stopped, I followed it with a left jab. The punching bag retreated, attempting to surrender. I waited until it returned for another round. Holding my hands up, I fixed my form, narrowing my shoulders and protecting my face.

Left. Right. Right. Left. Instead of relying solely on boxing, I let the momentum carry my body. Spinning, I came around, smacking the bag with my forearm. If it were a real person, I'd kick at their knee, snapping it before going in for a chokehold.

I had my fist drawn back, ready to strike it again when the bag begged for mercy. The last hit had cut through the fabric, and the sand inside fell to the floor. Inspecting my knuckles, I could see a fine dusting coating my hands.

The trainer waved at me to stop. "These damned bags are always breaking. You'd think with how much we charge you for membership, we'd replace them more regularly."

I gave him a slight nod before meandering back to the bench with my gym bag. My lungs were on fire, angry at how hard I was working out this morning. But if I was going to be a functional human being for the rest of the day, I had to let out some steam now.

I hated working out. Unfortunately, I loved food and with how much I ran my mouth, I needed a mean right hook to back it up. I could be in the weight room bulking up with the other steroid junkies, or in the yoga studio proving men with guts were incapable of touching their toes. Instead, I came to the older part of the gym with the retired vets lifting free weights and shadow boxing away their demons.

Chimes sounded from my gym bag and I searched for my phone. I didn't need to read the text to know it was Griffin apologizing for arriving at the gym late. It had become a sick game where I tried to convince him to work up a sweat, and he showed just in time for me to suggest breakfast.

Not today.

I texted him back to meet me in the locker room. Like always, he'd show up with a gym bag to sell the charade, but today I was going to find out if he bothered packing clothes. Throwing a towel around my shoulders, I snatched my gym bag and headed toward the men's locker room.

Through the lobby, I found Griff turning in circles. "Seriously, you don't even know where it is, do you?"

"I was waiting for you."

"Well then..." I take a slight bow. "After you then."

"Jerk."

I gave him a pat on the ass as I walked past, heading toward the back of the gym. As we passed the studios, the smell of chlorine grew stronger until we banked right into the locker rooms. Every once in a while, I'd get lucky and there'd be a bearish man with a towel wrapped around his waist, but today it looked like all the beef had opted to stay in bed.

"Are we really doing this? You look like you've already been working out. How about we call it a day and head to the HideOut?"

Called it. I turned toward the row of lockers, pulled one open and tossed my bag in. His eyes were attempting to burn a hole in the side of my head. "Nope. You're getting some exercise today that doesn't include Sebastian's cock."

"Don't be jealous that I'm getting my cardio outside of the gym."

I hated he was right. "We're hitting the pool. You can splash around while I swim laps."

"But Chad has a new omelet..."

"Then we can sit in the hot tub."

In the two years I had known Griffin, I had never seen him move so fast. Pants hit the tiles, and he was digging through his gym bag for shorts. When he finally pulled them out, I snatched the tag off the waistband. "Really? For how many months have these been in there?"

"Shut up."

Griffin was the newest addition to our troupe. There were times he grated on me with his comic book obsession and constantly yammering about superheroes, but he meant well. But out of the four of us, he was our source of culture. Alejandro was our sex fiend, Bernard our sagely dad, and me—I was the pragmatic one with a chip on my shoulder. The things that grated on me about Griffin were what made him a good friend, a calm to my chaotic frenzy.

"Want me to draw you a picture? It'll last longer?"

Standing in the buff, he rested his hands on his hips, baring every inch of himself. If this were a porno, I'd have him pinned against the lockers as I railed him to the sound of a silky smooth synthesizer. Eyeing his belly, the thought lingered. Thankfully, we swore off from hooking up with members of breakfast club. Instead, I snapped my towel, landing a sharp strike against his stomach.

He laughed as his eyes drifted south. "Got you hot and bothered, I see."

"Jerk."

We both let out a laugh as we changed and headed to

the pool. True to form, I got in a series of quick laps, cursing my inability to maintain my form. Griffin, on the other hand, doggy paddled back and forth, just enough to classify the event as physical activity. After finishing my twentieth lap, I hopped out of the pool to find him already enjoying the bubbles in the hot tub.

Level with the floor, I took my first step into the steaming water. Three more steps and it covered my waist. The chill of the pool vanished. I positioned myself in front of a series of jets that would massage the knot from the base of my back.

"Rough day?"

I nodded. "Try week."

"I saw the alerts on the HeroApp™. That was a full-on invasion. I've never seen so many heroes in one place."

"Do you know of a hero with four arms? Alien?" There was nobody more knowledgeable than Griffin when it came to superheroes. Part of his job required him to be familiar with them, but mostly, he was a geek.

"Four-Arms?"

"Nope. This one was green."

"Sentient Spider?"

"Nope. Eyes were more serpentine."

"Lizard Dude?"

"Now you're just making up names."

"Prometheus? Yellow and Black suit?"

I knew it. "Yup, that's the one."

"You got to meet Prometheus? The magazine has tried to get an interview with him for the last year."

"Do you know anything about him?"

"He arrived here from a parallel world. Rumor is his home planet took a different evolutionary turn. They're this crazy mix of technology and magic. Beyond that, everything is just hearsay. He wasn't part of a team and just randomly pops up when there's a global-level event. He once helped the Centurions stop the Ynieth shapeshifters from attacking Earth."

"I had to rescue him yesterday."

"That's so cool. I'm jealous you got to—"

The way he froze mid-sentence, I assumed my expression must have given away the outcome. There was a minute of silence before he switched sides in the hot tub, resting a steaming, moist hand on my shoulder. I nodded, thankful he didn't push the conversation.

"Were you there long?"

"I got sidelined after the first patient."

"Why?"

The bubbles worked at the knot in my back. If I didn't have to check-in at work, I could have sat there all day. As I let go of the tension in my muscles, I focused my attention on the bubbles breaking the surface of the water.

In the reflection, I could make out the shadowy figure staring back at me. Nonchalantly, I waved my arm through the image and it vanished, swallowed by the depths of the hot tub.

"Topic switch."

Breakfast club had a thousand rules, most of them we made and then immediately broke. However, the survival of our friendships relied on some boundaries. The moment I invoked one of the most sacred, Griffin moved on.

"Sebastian booked us a cabin up in the mountains. It started out as me asking him about camping."

I gave a nod with my head to suggest getting out. Griffin moved to the stairs as he spoke. "Nope, not happening. Too many bugs. Impossible to sleep. No menu options. He's a bit of a city boy. Yup, a couple of days roughing it in a cabin with only two bathrooms and a private chef. It'll be torture."

Walking the length of the pool, I tried to understand how he and Sebastian worked. I wasn't sure who was dating out of their league, but they weren't playing the same game.

We arrived at the lockers and I dropped my shorts while toweling off. "Oh, speaking of sexy men, do you or Sebastian know an Aiden at Revelations?"

"I only worked there a day, but Sebastian should. Why do you ask?"

"Oh, just somebody I bumped into." I pulled the towel over my head, giving it a quick wipe down. The perks of having a buzzed head, easy maintenance, and I always knew the moment it started raining.

I pulled on a pair of briefs and then my work pants. "I was going—"

"Aiden Scott," Griffin said. "Former blogger picked up by the magazine. He writes their online content." I hadn't even seen him grab his phone, but he was already scrolling through his texts.

"Remind me to never share secrets with you."

"Sebastian says he's a nice enough guy."

"You're getting stalkerish." The truth was, I wanted more information. Not only did I owe Aiden a thank you for saving my life, but I wouldn't mind seeing that scruffy face staring up at me as I plowed him.

"So you don't want his number?"

"Whoa. Whoa. Don't be crazy." Okay, so this morning, I'd be paying for Griffin's coffee. When my phone vibrated with a text message, I grinned. I had a moment imagining Aiden walking away from me and what he'd look like without jeans. Yeah, he'd be fun in the sack.

"If you're done daydreaming about wrecking one of Sebastian's employees, we're going to be late to breakfast."

I caught myself licking my lips, and it wasn't because of Chad's crepes.

"Bernard, are you okay?"

He stared at his coffee as if he was searching for answers to the universe. While Alejandro went on a tirade about the benefits of sleeping with a psychic, Bernard had been unusually quiet. At this point, the big guy would have been making dry, subtle quips about Alejandro's latest conquest.

"It's been a long night."

Cryptic. He was the last one at the table to beat around the bush. But when Chad stopped by the table, taking the cold cup of coffee, replacing it with a new one, complete with steam, he finally looked up. He worked himself to the bone, but the circles around his eyes spoke volumes.

"And then he predicted how I was going to finish him, and what do you know, he was right."

Shaking my head, I glared at Alejandro, who, in his usual self-indulgent way, missed reading the room. "Big guy, what's going on? First rule of—"

"Just a lot on my mind. Work has been rough this morning. It was an all-hands-on-deck situation after yester-day. The Centurions barely made it in time. It'll be another long day as we go through the casualties and reach out to the families."

"You call the families?" I assumed the Centurions were like the rest, swoop in, save the day, then sign a few photos before heading back to their posh base of operations.

Knowing they contacted the families made me hate them a little less.

"Each and everyone." That was the perk of being a paramedic. There was no doubt about my abilities in the ambulance, and I rarely thought about the patient after the fact. Every once in a while, I considered the specific ailments and what I could have done better, but it was about the medicine, not the patient.

I rested a hand on his shoulder, giving it a squeeze. "You're good people, Bernard."

"Well," Griffin started, "I have some news that will perk up the table." So help me God, if he announced a comic book release day again, I might very well slap him.

"Xander..." He turned to face me. "Our dear, dear friend Xander—"

"Griffin." The last person in the world I should have entrusted with a secret. I skipped thinking about how I'd kill him and focused on how I'd dispose of his body.

"Has himself a crush."

Alejandro let out a dramatic gasp. "Like a 'go out on a date' crush or 'I want to treat his ass like a buffet' crush?"

Even Bernard sipped his coffee with one eye in my direction. With a swift motion, I kicked Griffin under the table. Next time he joined me in the pool, I'd drown him. Being a paramedic, I could kill him and dispose of the body before anybody noticed he was missing.

"Ohhh." Alejandro's eyes went wide as he sat back.

"He's doing that murdery thing again. It's a 'go out to dinner' crush."

"Stop calling him a crush." I banged my fist on the table harder than expected. All three leaned back at the burst of anger. They held their tongues, waiting for me to process my actions.

"That was loud," I mumbled. "Sorry about that. But Alejandro..." I flung a sugar packet at him. "It's not a crush."

"The table says otherwise," Bernard said before diving into his coffee again. Leave it to my catastrophic love life to bring the man back to reality.

"I was at the bridge yesterday, and, well, I nearly died."

"Get past the boring parts," Griffin said.

"The bridge gave out under me, and I was hanging over the river by a piece of rebar."

"Drama," Alejandro added, "I love it."

Another kick under the table. He pushed his chair out of reach. He grabbed his avocado toast and started chomping. Sticking something in his mouth was the only way to pause the quips.

"Get on with it," Griffin said. "You were about to die and..."

Death. Hanging over the water, the chances of survival were almost zero, but I didn't think about dying. It wasn't a superhero that dove to save me. It was an ordinary man. Okay, maybe he wasn't all that ordinary.

"Out of nowhere, a hand reached out. It was this guy I bumped into on the bridge. He was there trying to get a story, I think. If it wasn't for him, I'm pretty sure I would have... died."

"So now you're going to reward him with some sweet loving?"

I lied. Alejandro wouldn't let a full mouth slow him down.

The thought had certainly crossed my mind. However, unlike Alejandro, my activities in the bedroom didn't get discussed as if they were the morning news. I wasn't a prude. I just didn't like everybody knowing how often I did... or didn't get laid.

"I owe him a thank you."

"And..." Not only was I going to drown Griffin, but I'd go after everybody in his family, too. Nobody would survive, thanks to his insistence on making me say it out loud.

"He wasn't harsh on the eyes."

All three of them smiled, grins stretching from ear to ear. Nope, I would not blush. There was no way I was going to let them know I had already thought about Aiden writhing underneath me.

"Is that his murder face?" asked Alejandro.

"No, that's more of a scrunched-up brow." Great, when Griffin and Alejandro got going, there was no stopping them.

"You mean like this?" Alejandro scrunched up his face.

Bernard joined the mockery. "No, it's more like this."

"Bernard," I growled. The man's scrunched-up face was dangerously accurate. I had to give him props. "Okay, that's not a terrible impression."

Griffin derailed their mocking and pointed to my work pants. "I thought they told you to take some time off. Are you going in?"

"I'm going in to change their minds."

Bernard put his hand on my wrist, a signature move that he was about to say something I should take to heart. "Maybe you need to take a few days off. It wouldn't hurt after the mayhem yesterday." Even though he spoke to me, the words seemed to be directed toward himself. How bad had it been at Centurion headquarters?

"That's weird." We all turned to Chad standing at the counter holding the Zipper's metal thermos. Like clockwork, the speedster arrived every morning to pick up his coffee before a day of heroing.

"He's never late," Griffin muttered.

That was my exit before Griffin started spitting out statistics about how fast Zipper could run. Standing up, I finished my coffee and tossed some money on the table.

"Wish me luck."

"Make sure you use plenty of lube, big boy."

I flipped off Alejandro as I exited the HideOut.

Staring at the text message with Aiden's phone number, I was surprised by how quickly Sebastian had relayed the information to Griffin. With gay men, they worked at lightning speed when they sniffed a potential connection. Between Aiden's number and the paycheck in my pocket, it made the awkward conversation with my boss bearable. At least I'd be able to go back to work tomorrow. Then I'd deal with the stares from my co-workers.

Now that I thought about it, I hadn't seen that many medics in the bay in years. It was as if the world had slept in and taken a deep breath. After yesterday's event, perhaps there'd be a slow period while heroes and villains alike licked their wounds.

The afternoon sun beamed down, leaving the day unusually warm for the end of summer. But with a cool breeze pushing against my face, I had to remind myself to smile. Once I deposited my paycheck, it'd be a Chinese takeout night and old martial arts films.

"It doesn't get much better than this," I muttered.

I neared the entrance of the bank to see several people running out. I had spoken too soon. A woman clutched her laptop bag as she ran past me. I stared at my phone and could see a red blip had appeared in the HeroApp™. While the heroes might have taken a day off, the villains had other plans.

I debated skipping the bank and heading home. As part of our health class in school, they had taught us to flee or hide when a superpowered battle broke out. Apparently, hiding under your desk would somehow stop mind control or lava monsters. Off duty, I usually avoided situations that might require me to work, but today I felt like pressing my luck.

Standing at the giant brass turnstile door, I squinted, trying to get a look inside. There were dozens of people lying on the floor while others hid behind massive marble columns. Try as I might, I couldn't find the source of their panic.

So, in I went.

They had built the lobby of the bank to impress. A large room with towering columns that directed patrons through a two-story arch into the main part that held the tellers. There was shouting from somewhere inside, multiple voices demanding the other hurry. I crouched next to a man in a business suit, using the column as a shield.

"How many?"

His eyes had glassed over as he hugged himself. "Six."

"Powers?"

"Mr. Mad," he mumbled.

A low-level villain, he rarely managed a caper before one of the local heroes kicked the crap out of them. I flipped to the distress screen and tapped the "In Distress" button, adding information about the culprit. It'd be a minute or two before Zipper or Cobalt appeared. The fight would be over before it started.

"They're not coming," he added.

"Soon as you can, make it to the door. Get out of here." I wasn't going to square off against a lunatic and his heavily armed goons in raccoon masks, but I could at least lower the body count.

Peeking around the corner, I spotted one man in their signature red and white striped shirts. I patted the man on the shoulder the moment the gunman turned his back toward the entrance. "Go."

He started in a crawl and quickly climbed to his feet, looking over his shoulder. He was out the door and safe. It wasn't much, but it was one less target for them to shoot.

Pulling up the HeroApp™, I clicked the distress button again, searching the map for any local hero sightings. "Figures," I mumbled. They were everywhere, parading around all day, but when they were needed to actually protect people, there wasn't a hero to be found.

A blip caused my phone to vibrate. "Hellcat, really? There must be another dimensional rift nearby." She wasn't a slouch in the rescuing department, but unlike the majority of heroes, she didn't possess super strength or the ability to teleport. No, our only protector was a woman with a black belt and a grudge.

"Gimme your wallet."

Dammit. I had been so concerned with the criminals in

the bank I hadn't seen this one sneak around the column. Pressing my back against the marble, I scooted upward. Crouched on the floor meant my options were limited. If I could—

"Don't move another muscle."

"Or what?"

"I don't want to kill you, man. Just give me your wallet."

"I'm going to reach into my pocket…"

Lunging, I grabbed the barrel of his shotgun. Pushed high, he wouldn't be able to shoot me in the face. Small victories. I tried clocking him in the face with my left hand, but he pulled backward. My hand slipped as he jerked the gun free. Through the raccoon mask, his eyes twitched, preparing for—

BANG.

The shot lifted me off my feet, hurling me across the floor until another column stopped my sliding. Without thinking, I patted down my chest, ready to assess the damage. My shirt had dozens of tiny holes scattered across my chest and stomach. Shoving my finger into a dime-sized gap in the cloth, there were no holes in my skin, no blood. If I hadn't sailed across the lobby, I might suspect he missed, but the Swiss cheese shirt told a different story.

The bandit had frozen in shock, giving away his rookie status within Mr. Mad's operation. Was that the first time he fired on an innocent? I didn't care about his answer, because it was about to be his last.

Hardly an ache. I crawled to my feet, standing up so Mr. Raccoon could see the tattered remains of my shirt. As I stalked toward him, he hardly moved, the barrel swaying slightly from the shivering of his arms. He was scared, and rightfully so.

Intentional or not, his finger tightened, and he fired again. I ducked low, lunging so that my arms wrapped around his waist. We tumbled, the crook landing hard on his ass. I moved quickly, climbing up his body until I straddled his chest. My first punch knocked off his mask. The second knocked blood from his lip. The bastard had shot me. No, he tried to *kill* me. It was the sixth punch when his body relaxed and his face transformed into a bloody mess. Not dead, but he'd be hurting for weeks to come.

"Ahem."

Standing only a few feet away was a vigilante, a woman in head-to-toe leather. She pulled back her hood, revealing neon pink hair. The thin mask covering her eyes shouldn't have hidden her identity, but heroes were good about squirreling away their alter-egos. Her eyes ran up and down my body, hovering at my fists covered in the criminal's blood. Hellcat was known for her brutality in a fight. She carefully studied me, deciding if I was the threat.

"He tried to kill me."

"You need to get out of here before the cops show."

"I can't flee the scene of a crime."

"You better if you don't want them figuring out your identity."

Being a paramedic meant I knew a good number of Vanguard's police force. The moment they saw me, they'd know me by name, and without my uniform, it'd be obvious that it was a day off. Her words didn't make—

I eyed my t-shirt. "Oh. Damn."

"Rookie mistake," she said. "And right now, there's not enough of us for careless errors."

Us?

Hellcat walked by me, and with a slap on the ass, she bolted into the lobby. The gunfire started, a few screams, but mostly men grunting and the occasional cheer.

I eyed my shirt again. Us. I was one of them, a damned superhero. I did the only thing I could as the sirens grew louder, I ran for the door.

6

THE FOG FROM YESTERDAY HAD BARELY LIFTED. THE ENTIRE scene at the bank felt like a distant memory. When I returned home, I had spent plenty of time scrubbing the blood off my hands, standing in the shower, trying to dissect what Hellcat had said. Heroes were the bane of Vanguard, and I never hesitated in saying we'd be better off without them. Perhaps the stress of the situation had distorted my memory?

A shirt riddled with bullet holes rested on my coffee table. The evidence didn't lie.

I plopped down on the couch. I had yet to do more than slide on a pair of briefs before making coffee. The steaming cup was the only thing that mattered in the world in this moment. It was all in my head, but the moment I took the first sip, the energy pulsed through my body. I'm a coffee slut, so sue me.

My phone vibrated, and I prayed it wasn't the HeroApp™ reporting another robbery. Normally I was ready to jump into action and head to work, but today, my head was elsewhere.

Emergency.

I didn't recognize the number. After a restless night of sleep, I prepared a long string of swears that would make a sailor blush. As my thumb hovered over the send button, the tiny rectangle shook again.

A: Sorry. It's Aiden.

X: You scum-sucking telemarketing douche bag cum guzzler.

I swore my heart struggled to climb through the gaps in my ribcage, thumping hard enough my eardrums pulsed. There was no way "sorry" would quite cover it. Oh yes, thank you for saving my life, by the way, I think you're a—

A: At least one of those things is correct. No, he did not end the text message with a wink. I nearly choked on my tongue, unsure if I should snort or sigh with relief.

X: Sorry, I thought you were a telemarketer. Didn't know it was a handsome man hitting me up.

A: Grif gave me your number.

X: He mentioned Sebastian knew you.

"Xander." I stood, pacing back and forth across the living room. "You have a delete key. Use it. You sound like a barbarian. Why not just send him a dick pic?" The thought crossed my mind, but perhaps I should wait until the second conversation.

X: Emergency? What's up?

Business. Assess the situation. Remove the emotion. Look for the problem. Examine avenues toward a solution. If only I could apply my paramedic training to every aspect of my life. Perhaps I wouldn't be an angry man ready to punch holes in the wall.

A: They're gone.

X: Who?

Let me guess, the mayor, victim of another clandestine organization of villains looking to empty the bank vaults. No, I'm pretty sure that was last month. The nuclear power plant? Wait, I saved the Winged Warrior after he got hit by a not-so-deadly death ray. In Vanguard City, emergencies were more common than jaywalkers.

A: The heroes. They're gone. Every. One. Of. Them.

The pacing stopped, my feet half on the rug, half on the cheap linoleum flooring. Slowly, I turned until I eyed the t-shirt peppered with tiny holes. It made little sense. Hellcat had arrived at the bank.

"There's not enough of us." Her words had sounded like a warning yesterday. Did she know about the missing heroes? Sure, one or two would go vanishing as their alter ego visited their mother in Kansas, but not all of them. Hellcat arriving at the bank proved there were...

"Xander, you're an idiot." I had mocked the alert on my phone, wondering why the only person swinging into action at the bank was a second-string hero. But unlike the vast majority of heroes gifted with cosmic power, alien abilities, or drawing on the supernatural, she was an everyday woman with a mean left-hook.

X: **How do you know?**

A: **Reporter. I notice things.**

X: **Why message me?**

A: **You're the only studly medic I know saving superheroes.**

X: **So you know other studly medics?** Ha. Alejandro would give me a high-five for that one. How that man turned on the charm with such ease was beyond me. He could have a new man in bed every night, and here I was attempting to pull my foot out of my mouth.

A: **Only one who owes me a favor.**

My heart sank. The playful banter had taken a wicked turn and landed squarely on a tit-for-tat situation. I plopped down on the couch, staring at the text. He wasn't wrong. Saving my life put me in his debt. I had hoped to repay him by burying my face between the cheeks of his ass. This was less fun.

A: **I figure you at least owe me a coffee. We can negotiate the rest of the date.**

X: **Date?**

A: **I don't save every damsel in distress I come across.**

"Okay, just for that, I'm not using lube." Even *I* couldn't fight the grin spreading across my face. I tried to push my lips down, refusing to start my day off in a good mood. Despite my best attempts, the smile stuck, and I went back to imagining the thick reporter bent over my couch.

X: I *am* an adorable damsel.

A: That you are. Let me know if you notice anything?

X: Only because you called me pretty.

A: ;)

For a moment, the craziness at the bank ceased to exist. I didn't care about the lack of heroes or the shirt turned Swiss cheese. Right now, the only thing that mattered was a flirtatious man who deserved a proper thank you. After a proper thanks, I wanted to give him a very improper thanks.

I reached into my underwear, recalling the bulge of muscle on the man's arm as he reached down to save me. The dusting of hair creeping toward his wrist would be an amazing sight reaching into my briefs. After being on the receiving end of his grip, I could only imagine how firm it'd be as his fingers circled the shaft of my cock.

Pulling the skin back, the head pressed firmly against the stitching, refusing to relent until I took care of business. I closed my eyes, leaning back, settling in for a morning of taunting and teasing my cock. I didn't have any place to be until work, and I'd be a lot more agreeable if I came.

I reached deeper, giving my balls a firm tug. The

thought of them slapping against Aiden's ass was more than enough to make it jerk upright. Dragging my finger over the slit, the precum had flowed, an unusual occurrence unless a guy spent quality time servicing my package.

The moment I imagined him on all fours, his jeans hiked down past his ass, the only thing between me and my goal, a pair of white undies. Sliding them down, I could almost imagine the heat of his ass as I pressed myself against him, teasing the man.

"Fuck," I moaned. The image of his ass opening for my cock, hands holding his hips, guiding him back—

My toes curled and I let out a low growl. The sensation spread across my lap, working down my sack, across my taint, feeling like an electric current running down my legs. I came hard enough that the tiny drop of precum on my underwear turned into a wet patch. Pinching the base, I milked my cock, shaking out the last of the cum.

Panting, I slid my hand from the waistband, wiping the evidence of Aiden's hotness on my briefs. I'd have told anybody that it took forever for me to finish, but perhaps all I needed was the proper motivation. Motivation in the form of a chubby reporter with an annoyingly charming personality.

Apparently, I had some free time for breakfast.

"I'm just going to come out and say it." I pointed at Griff first, then at Alejandro, and finally at Bernard. "No, you know what, you're part of this too." My finger extended toward Chad as he poured another cup of coffee for Bernard. "You're all acting like somebody pissed in your Cheerios."

The entire coffee shop was quietly whispering. Everybody ignored their steaming beverages as they traded theories about what might have happened. A nearby couple had their phones out as they doom scrolled through the newsfeeds, reporting a lack of superheroes. It was perhaps the greatest event to happen in the world, and considering how often intergalactic armies arrived to enslave us, that was saying something.

Alejandro I understood. For a man who worked in a club catering to superheroes, his clientele had dried up overnight. Even Bernard's job with the Centurions could be in jeopardy. Now that he thought about it, without people saving the planet, Griffin might not have a job anymore. It was the first time that I realized that each of us had a connection to the powered community through our occupations.

"And what about you?" I'm sure my eyes narrowed as I directed my gaze at Chad. "Why are you all sorts of moody?"

The barista's face turned white. For the first time in his life, he didn't have a quip. Nervously, he laughed. "You know Zipper leaves me hundred dollar tips, right? How else do I afford lavish vacations with the hubby?"

Lies. What he was fibbing about, I wasn't sure, but I'd circle back to that conversation the next time he tried to set me up with his cousin.

"You must be happy," Griffin said.

I raised my eyebrow, not at the statement but at the tone. The usual upbeat plucky character in our ensemble sounded more like me, an undercurrent of annoyance and anger.

"Care to elaborate?"

"You're the one who hates supers. The rest of us are content to co-mingle in a world filled with heroes, but you..." His voice had turned low, almost to where I expected the next words to be a scolding insult. "There isn't a day where you didn't wish they'd vanish."

Bernard and Alejandro were unusually quiet. I wouldn't have thought getting my wish would drive a wedge between us. Yes, their jobs depended on heroes, but so did mine. Perhaps after a day or two, they'd see that the people of Vanguard were resilient enough to hold their own.

"I'm not sure where you're going with this. Are you blaming me? Or are you mad that for a change, I'm not the one on the losing side of this argument?"

Griffin leaned back in his chair, withholding any follow-up statement. I didn't speak up when he went off about a new comic book. With Alejandro, I never judged him being a hero chaser. Good for him. Bernard, well, he was Bernard.

"I'm not going to sit here and cheer that my argument won. I'm not a dick. But give it a couple days. Maybe you'll see that I was right, and we can get along without superheroes."

Bernard started shaking his head. For years he had worked with the Centurions, one of the world's elite super-hero teams. He always had interesting stories to tell about events happening behind the scenes. There was even a time when I had one of his team in the back of my ambu-lance after being impaled on a beam of light.

"It's going to descend into chaos," Bernard muttered.

"I wouldn't—"

Every phone in the coffee shop dinged at the same time. Without a doubt, it was the HeroApp™. Nobody at the table reached for their phone. Their willingness to ignore their devices caused my anxiety to jump. Gay men were wired to their phones. We'd have them installed in our brains if we could.

"Fine, I'll bite." I flipped mine over and, of course, it was the HeroApp™. See, everything was returning to normal. There were plenty of blips on the— Where the heroes were typically identified by red dots, the map showed nearly a dozen black dots all over the city, including the Ward.

The heroes were gone, but the villains, on the other

hand, didn't seem to be suffering. There were no red blips appearing, no heroes, none.

"Chaos," Bernard said as he got up from his chair. "I have to head to work and see what the government is going to do. Be careful out there. Better yet, check in every few hours."

Alejandro nodded. "Si, Papi."

Bernard's face hardened as he looked at me. I could handle nearly dying or being covered in gore, but under his disapproving gaze, something in my stomach tightened. Up to this point, our difference of opinion had been light-hearted and playful, but now the guilt forced me to sink into my chair.

"Be careful," I echoed.

7

"Do you think it was the government?"

It took a moment before Lei smacked me on the shoulder, nearly knocking the coffee from my hand. I had been staring at my phone for the better part of twenty minutes, waiting for Aiden to return a text message. For the past few days, he had continued texting, keeping me informed about his investigation into the missing superheroes. Well, more like he complained about the lack of leads and no information to be had.

"The government? No, I don't think so. What would they have to gain?"

"You're way more fun when you're not deep dicking a man."

I spat, barely able to keep from choking on the coffee. Slowly, I turned my head to see the devious grin. I might be the burly, large and in-charge type of guy, but Lei was the one who lacked censorship.

"What?"

"Don't play me, fool. You're staring at that phone like you're waiting to find out if you won the lottery. I know when a medic is chasing skirt. Trousers? Kilts? What exactly is it you chase?"

"I don't."

"The death grip on your phone says otherwise."

"Have I mentioned how much I hate you?"

"This hour? Wait, did you mention it when you said hello?"

"You're exhausting."

"I'm pretty sure you said it when—"

"What do I have to say to stop this conversation?"

"His name."

"Aiden."

"I took you more for a Marcus. Maybe a Deshawn."

Lei would continue to take her jabs. Messing with me was her primary job, and she was more skilled at sarcasm than being a medic. She was a riot most of the time until her boredom turned toward me and she poked the bear. I enjoyed a good ribbing, but she had a knack for getting under the skin. Being partnered with her was my ticket into heaven… if I didn't kill her.

I couldn't argue with her. My mind was altogether else-where. Aiden was a pleasant distraction, something to take my mind away from the incident at the bank. I couldn't explain what had happened, how the bullets hadn't torn through my skin. Backpedaling through the events leading up to it, it all came down to Prometheus' death in the back of the ambulance.

I rubbed the bandage on my left arm. I probably should have tested it with a needle before using a box cutter. Not only did it leave a nasty gash I had to stitch myself, the throbbing pain reminded me I was anything but a superhero.

"Supervillain," I mumbled, returning to the conversation.

"Where?"

I held up my phone. "Aiden." For a fledgling reporter, he certainly took his job seriously. He hoped to crack this story and launch his career. Unfortunately, the next message was about as soul-crushing as they came.

A: Vex took me off the story. Another reporter got the assignment. Bleh.

X: Want me to beat up Vex?

"Oh dear God," Lei said. "You even grin while you're texting him." She reached down to her belt, tearing at the velcro, peeling it back as she wiggled about, trying to pull it through the loops.

"What are you doing?"

"I'm going to strangle myself. This is not okay. I like my

Xander full of piss and vinegar. Xander in love, I can't bear it."

A: **Dude is pretty damned scary. Think you can win?**

X: **I haven't thrown a fist where I didn't win.**

A: **Anger management issues. Noted.**

I think the text message was him being playful. Did he think I was angry enough that it'd be a problem? Okay, perhaps I yelled far more than was appropriate. But it wasn't like I had punched anybody, at least not in the last week.

A: **He believes it's a villain. Government contact says they're scrambling to prepare for whatever comes next.**

"What does he have to say? Do they know which villain did it? I bet it was Backtrack. He's always trying to change the past. What about Pagania? She opened that portal to Hell once? Oh God, do you remember that? Everything smelled of sulfur."

The memory alone caused a foul stench, forcing me to wrinkle my nose. "I had ash in my socks for a week."

Lei and I had seen some weird shit over the years. I might have gripes with superheroes, but it allowed me to experience some unusual things. Except, now without heroes, we sat across the street from a bagel shop, praying that a vigilante broke a bone and called for help.

"He's been chasing leads since it started and nothing. I'm rooting for him. A solid article like that could land him his dream job."

"Listen to you." She jabbed me in the arm. "You're sweet on him. And here I thought you just swapped photos in jockstraps."

I snorted. Not because she was wrong. I had spent yesterday posing in front of a mirror taking photos of just that. I hadn't worked up the courage to send them. Hard to be playful when the world was in crisis. Maybe tonight I'd give him a taste of what he'd get in the bedroom.

X: Stay safe out there.

A: Aww. You care.

X: I still owe you coffee.

A: Don't lie. You're going to guzzle that coffee fast so you can get to dessert.

Screw it. I had nothing to lose. With a couple of clicks, there was a photo of me in a jockstrap. Perhaps a few too many pounds, but with some creative flexing, there were shadows proving I had abs. Sort of. I clicked send and dropped the phone in my lap.

"I have no idea what you did with Xander, but this." Lei waved her hand around my face. "I don't know what to do with a boy and his puppy dog love."

"You know, I've figured out why you're single."

"Men get scared that I have bigger balls."

I was about to comment on her ability to drive a man to skydive without a parachute when my phone shook. It rested on my knee, and apparently I waited too long to answer. Lei's arm snapped with lightning speed, stealing my phone before I could stop her. She turned it long enough that it recognized my face and opened.

I rolled my eyes and leaned my head back. There was no use in climbing across the ambulance and strangling her. If that had been an option, it'd have happened months ago.

"First. Nice package. You have my respect. And it looks like I'm not the only one."

"What did he say?"

"I might be reading between the lines, but I think he wants to go bobbing for meat popsicles. I can't say I blame him. Jesus, what do you feed that thing? Miracle grow?"

"What did he say!" Okay, yelling wasn't the best idea. Now she knew how interested I was in Aiden's response. I'd be hearing about this for weeks to come.

"If I wasn't covering this stupid concert, I'd say let's skip coffee." She thrust the phone into my hand. "Rude of him to not at least send a photo of him in a leather harness. You guys do that, right?"

There was no point in protesting. I had taken those photos yesterday as well.

"Mass casualty incident at Vanguard concert hall. All available units respond to stage lot C. PD will advise when secure," barked dispatch.

"We're ignoring that, right?" I didn't want to beg.

"Fine, let's go save your piece of ass," she said, firing up the engine. Once in a great while, I remembered why I chose her as my partner.

This was a stretch of bad luck, determined to make my life miserable. Now we needed to barrel into a concert filled with thousands of people and hope somebody, anybody, arrived to stop it from turning into a bloodbath.

She yanked the seatbelt and as soon as it clicked, she turned the key. "Let's go save your man."

I didn't hate that thought. My man.

Thankfully, she didn't see me blush.

I licked the chocolate from my fingers. Leave it to the nurses to always make sure there were snacks in the break room. Holding my hand under a bottle of disinfectant, I waited for the clear liquid and then massaged it into my hands. Okay, I was officially ready to go back into the field.

Lei leaned over the reception desk, talking to the nurse. She was describing the concert and the sheer terror on people's faces. It had been difficult to tell if they were fleeing the scene, climbing over one another, or if they were attempting to tear each other apart. I had never witnessed chaos at that level.

This job had its share of weird, but this left me scratching my head. With thousands of people at the concert, the chances of finding Aiden were low. I left him a final text, asking him to be careful. He had responded with, "No guts, no glory." I wanted to call him an idiot. But it sounded dangerously similar to what I would have said, and I'm a smart guy. Sometimes.

"Come on, Lei. It's going to be a long day."

Lei reached out, bumping knuckles with the woman behind the counter. How she went from brash and rough around the edges to turning on the charm never ceased to amaze. The moment she turned in my direction, she froze. Her eyes widened as she leaned to the side, carefully inspecting something between me and the entrance to the emergency room.

"Villain?"

She shook her head.

"Hot man?"

Her head nodded slowly.

"My hot, or your hot?"

"Boy has some meat around his bone. He's everything—"

"Xander?" I almost didn't recognize the voice. I turned slowly, unsure of why Aiden might be at the hospital yet again. We really needed to work on our meeting locations.

"Is that him?" Lei whispered, leaning against my back. "Now I see why you edited those photos so much, big boy."

"Go to the truck. I'll be out in a moment."

"Not a chance in—"

I shot her a look that made it clear there was no negotiating. As she gave me the once over, I could almost hear her debating if she could take me in a fight. My biceps were as thick as her throat, and even then, I'd most likely bet on her.

"What are you doing here?"

"I hadn't even gotten into the concert when a trio of villains showed up. It's the first big event in Vanguard since the depowering. I knew something was going to happen."

"You went looking for trouble?"

"I don't remember you complaining when I saved your life." Try as I might, I couldn't argue with that logic. I'd certainly try, but it'd be a losing battle.

"I, uh..." I ran my hand across the stubble on my skull. Each day I made a thousand decisions, resulting in people living or dying, but nothing was harder than showing even the tiniest bit of gratitude. Much like the photo, it was time to pull the trigger and deal with the fallout later. "Thank you. You know, for saving me. I'd be dead if it wasn't for you."

"Some heroes wear capes, others..." he gestured in my direction. I was many things, but a hero wasn't one of them. While the heroes hid and licked their wounds, I still had a job to do. Not all of us had the luxury of an alter ego.

"Are we finally going to nail down that coffee date?"

I appreciated his determination. My schedule was generally a nightmare, and it appeared his wasn't much better. Two men married to their jobs. Nothing about this was going to end well. We couldn't manage a thirty-minute lunch date over a hot beverage and I was sitting here thinking... what was I thinking? When did I go from imagining him naked to giggling like a schoolgirl?

"Xander?"

"Tonight? I get—"

"No." His voice was barely audible, as if he were trying to share a secret he didn't want anybody to hear. "Turn around slowly."

"If you wanted to see my ass, I have photos."

"Xander."

The second time he used my name, there was a distinct lack of emotion. I followed his gaze past my shoulder. It took a moment before I saw the receptionist Lei had been speaking with. She had frozen in place, but it was the dark orbs that replaced her eyes that were unsettling. The vibrant nurse had vanished, and now she resembled something from a horror movie.

"There's more of them."

Aiden stopped being subtle. Pointing to a doctor, and then a patient on a gurney, each of them suffered the same affliction. The more I looked about the emergency room, the more it appeared to be spreading.

"We need to get to the door," I whispered.

I grabbed Aiden's hand, ready to bolt for the exit. Three security guards blocked our path, each of them dark-eyed. I debated on charging through them, even with their hands resting on their weapons. I might be able to withstand a few slugs, but I couldn't put Aiden at risk.

"They're not moving," he whispered.

The room filled with whispers from the frozen people. The sounds coming from their mouths came in breathy gasps. None of their mouths moved as they attempted to speak. The effect made the entire lobby sound like a creepy echo chamber.

"How much longer till I see a doctor?" A man yelled from the sitting area.

Before he could leave the waiting room, one of the security guards jumped on him. Others screamed, but it was nearly impossible to tell who was normal and who had become possessed. The emergency room descended into chaos as people scrambled for the exit.

"Follow me." I pulled Aiden close, pinching his elbow to guide him away from the anarchy. The last time we touched, I had nearly died, and now it happened again. I was wondered if the world was trying to give us a hint.

I spent more than my share of time in the hospital. The primary hallways were only part of the labyrinth of corridors used by the staff. If people were going to tear into one another, I wanted away. After being shot, I didn't think they could hurt me, but the box cutter left me with doubts. I also couldn't risk Aiden. I was going to get that coffee date one way or another.

"Crap." We had barely gone twenty feet when a security

guard blocked the door leading away from the emergency room. We slowed, and I turned around, ready to drag Aiden out another way.

At the entrance to the hospital, a man stepped through the automated doors. The chances a guy dressed in all black without a face happened to be a superhero were low. The trench coat of billowing smoke and the lines of dark clouds pouring off his head all pointed toward villain.

I knew the figure, but I couldn't—the bridge. His arms weren't as lengthy, and he had replaced the talons with smoky hands, but it was him. This time, I wouldn't be able to rely on Lei mowing him down with the truck.

"What now?" asked Aiden.

"I choose guard," I said.

"Dude has a gun," Aiden said.

I noticed that. An average person with a gun didn't worry me as much as the dude with smoke for a face. A woman screamed, running in our direction with her fingers poised to scratch my eyes. Before she reached us, Aiden jabbed her in the throat, dropping the attacker.

"I'm impressed." Impressed and turned on. As a trio of nurses wrestled with a doctor, it was not the time to think with my cock. Whatever madness had spread through the hospital, I had to assume it had something to do with Mr. Monochrome.

"I'm going for the guard. Moment he's down, run down

the hall. Past the nurse's station, there's an exit that should get you to the parking lot."

"But—"

"I'm not asking."

The guard's eyes had turned black, consumed by whatever madness seeped into the hospital. I didn't want to slug the guy, but if it got us out of here, I'd slap him and his mom. His hand fidgeted with his holster, his fingers not as nimble as normal.

Jumping over a man in a hospital gown, I threw my arms out wide, ready to tackle the guard just as he freed his gun. Twenty pounds lighter, I took him off his feet. We hit the ground, and I didn't waste time yelling at Aiden. "Run!"

He ran toward the swinging doors and hesitated while I attempted to bat the gun out of the guard's hand. "Go, I'll be right behind you." I slugged the man under me, less concerned with him and more with the supervillain waltzing through the emergency room.

Aiden vanished, and as the doors swung back and forth, I could see him bolting. A few seconds later, the gun fired. The tip of the weapon rested against my shoulder, and like before, I could feel the impact of the bullet. No pain. I didn't wait for a second shot. One punch, two, three, and on the pull back for a fourth, the guard's body went limp.

"Stay down," I mumbled.

"Can it be? A hero?"

I rolled off the guard to see the villain had worked his way across the lobby. His leather jacket moved awkwardly until I figured out it was smoke wafting into the air. Even his head, features hidden in the black, rose off his shoulders like he was composed of fumes. Half a dozen of the black-eyed citizens of Vanguard stood at his back, a squad of backup dancers ready to put on a show.

"I'm not a hero," Xander barked.

"Not for long."

8

With a simple swat from the back of his hand, he sent me flying across the emergency room. The reception desk broke my fall and, quite possibly, one of my ribs. A man that thin should *not* be that strong. Before I could make sure my bones were pointing in the right direction, one of his crazed nurses jumped on me.

I braced my forearm against her throat, keeping her at bay as she snarled. A beefy gal, she should have weighed more or at least required some effort to stop her chomping teeth from sinking into my cheek. My knuckles connected with her jaw and she flew off, rolling into the uncomfortable waiting room chairs.

"Take that, hose beast." The days in the gym had paid off.

The man in the trench coat paused his approach, eyeing the woman lying on the floor. I had a moment of worry. Did I kill her? Was she savable? Oh God, what had I done? Staring at my hands, I quickly realized that being bulletproof might not be the only ability Prometheus had bestowed upon me.

"You're not depowered." He sounded shocked at the revelation. "When I'm done with you, perhaps I'll find your friend." The man's voice had a chalky quality, as if he'd spent most of his youth sipping whisky and smoking cigars. It made me want to punch him even harder. Okay, everything made me want to punch somebody. This time it'd be justified.

"Ass clown, if you go near him, I'll tear out your insides." I let out a sigh of relief as the nurse rolled onto her back, shaking her head. When she sat upright, she checked her limbs, then patted down her chest. She had returned to normal. Once I knew the rules of the game, I could play.

"You and what army? You can't even handle my faithful followers." Griffin was right, give a villain a chance to talk and they're going to spew some cryptic bullshit. His love of superheroes might actually be an asset right now. I needed to give Aiden time to get away.

"What's your name? I want to know what to put on your tombstone." This punk had ruined my shift, and somebody was going to be on the receiving end of my rage. It might as well be a villain. I was starting to understand why heroes got such a thrill from bashing bad guys.

The people in the room, still consumed by his influence, stopped fighting. They moved as one, standing upright and turning to face me. The man, with smoky wisps emanating from his head, quickly became the least scary thing in the room. I could drive my knuckles into him, but his minions, it was harder to justify hurting innocent people.

"Smoke," they said in unison.

"Really? Smoke? You could pick any name from the evil monicker playbook, and you chose Smoke?" Mocking the bad guy might not be the smartest move, but by now, Aiden should be running through the parking lot.

I slid off the nurses' station, careful as I put weight on my legs. Being thrown should have left bruises, or at least sore spots where they'd eventually form. But right now, blood pumped through my veins and I felt the best I had in a long time.

"A neophyte." As he tilted his head back, laughing, his duster fluttered. Everything about him was covered in smoke; even his clothes appeared as if they were burning. Okay, he could turn people into zombies, hit hard, and dress himself like an 80s goth. Got it.

"Why not control everybody?" The question put a stop to his laughing. "Oh," I laughed, "somebody has limitations." Griffin would slap me for mocking a villain. But it's not like an alien had made *him* bulletproof.

Smoke came at me, not running, but feet sliding along the floor. His hands were poised to snatch me by the neck. Driving my knuckles into his face was instinct, more than an intentional act. It landed with enough force that he never reached my throat. He staggered backward, and I rushed in.

I was going to kill him. Years of boxing at the gym would finally pay off. I jabbed him in the mouth before stepping into my cross. Knuckles passed through his face. The second jab ended short, his hand wrapping around my fist.

It shouldn't be possible, at least not for an average human, but the bones in my hand ground together. The jab to his kidney wasn't enough to hurt, but he loosened his grip. I reached for his neck, but my hand passed harmlessly through the darkness.

"What the—"

Smoke vanished in a puff of... well, smoke. Hands wrapped around my neck from behind and somebody kicked my knee, knocking my legs out from under me. As I swiped over my head, hoping to strike the villain, I couldn't feel anything.

"Quite sad, really," he mocked.

It felt like a train slammed into my back. The world spun, and I covered my head a second before slamming into the wall. The plaster fell as I drilled into the concrete. A stream of black shot out of the villain's hands, holding me in place, pushing me deeper into the wall.

The smoky beam held me in place, and for the first time, I could feel the pain in my chest. Pushing with both hands, I blocked the onslaught of black. Aiden should have gotten free, and hopefully, he continued to run far away from the building. This jerk had ruined a perfectly good encounter with the journalist.

I was pissed.

The skin around my fingertips turned a bright orange, then yellow. The black pushed back as the light in my palms grew brighter. It was bad enough Smoke interrupted what could have turned into plans for coffee. It was another thing entirely that he threatened the cub. He'd pay for even thinking about it.

A lick of fire grew from my forearm before receding into my skin. With another push forward, the light about my arms ignited. The first wave of fire reached my fingertips before vanishing.

"You can't win."

I flipped my hands over, the energy hammering me against the wall again. The glow around my hands didn't fade, but so help me God, becoming a human night light wouldn't save the day. Smoke's pummeling went from irritating to painful. From underneath my rolled sleeves, a black and gold film coated my arms until it wrapped about my hands. With a final flick of the wrists, the fire spread along my skin.

"I am going to—"

"Shut the hell up." Palms forward, the fire cut through the smoke, crossing the emergency room. Smoke's hands went up, attempting to protect his face. Fire washed around his body. Did it do damage? He didn't appear hurt, but it was enough for the moment. I preferred being close as I knocked the teeth out of his mouth.

I stepped away from the wall, flames continuing to roll along my forearms, crawling upward until the paramedic uniform caught fire and burned away. Underneath, a leather suit hugged my body, as if it had been tailored to my curves. It was cheesy, but it'd hide the blood when I crushed Smoke's skull.

Prometheus had passed along the gift of fire. It almost seemed *too* on the nose. Bulletproof and fire, okay, I could handle this. I just had to break every bone in the jerk who threatened Aiden, and then—

"Get him!" Smoke's voice was overly confident.

The dark-eyed minions of Smoke moved in unison. I didn't want to hurt innocent people in the hospital, but if I had to break a few bones to get at Smoke, it was a price they'd have to pay. If he thought a few lackeys would slow me, he had another thing coming.

"Backup is here." A blur of purple tackled a doctor, somersaulting as she hit the ground. She spun about on a foot, knocking the legs out from a nurse before they responded. An uppercut, a pivot and heel to a patient, and a punch to a security officer's jaw. She had dispatched Smoke's minions in a matter of seconds. It took a moment before I identified my sidekick.

"Hellcat," she said. The woman's purple mask covered her eyes. Between that and the black makeup coating her eyelids, it made it difficult to imagine who was underneath. Was it a homemade costume or did she have the number of Vanguard's superhuman tailor?

Pointing at my hands, she raised an eyebrow. "Powers?"

I nodded. Twice she appeared in the nick of time. Unlike the superheroes, she didn't leave a wake of destruction. I might not be a fan of those who controlled the weather or hurled vehicles in a fight, but vigilantes seemed to have their priorities in line.

"I'm going to kill—" Smoke had vanished. The people under his influence were already returning to normal. Hellcat helped a young nurse off the floor. Dammit, I let the man get away. I hardly noticed the pain as my knuckles drove into the hospital wall, punching a hole through the concrete. I had a grudge to settle, and I wouldn't be happy until I beat the smug expression off Smoke's face.

Had Aiden reached safety? I needed to text him to be sure. Reaching for my pocket, I realized my phone had burned away with my clothes. I let out a low growl as I slammed my palm into the wall. Several concrete blocks dislodged, flying into the parking lot. Lei stood in the parking lot, her eyes wide as the block landed a few feet away.

"Calm down. You need to go," Hellcat whispered.

"Not until I find—"

"You're the only powered hero..." she paused and corrected herself. "Person... in the city. You're in no shape to answer questions. Get out of here, and for the love of God, don't let anybody know who you are."

Wait, she didn't recognize me? I touched my face and could feel the texture of the suit covering my eyes and nose. Whatever spawned these gifts, they were doing a good job of keeping me and my identity safe. I had questions. Why did Smoke attack the hospital? Where had he gone? But most of all, I worried he could identify Aiden and put him in jeopardy. But I pushed them aside. Right now, as the sirens grew louder, I needed a place to hide.

"Rookie." She patted me on the shoulder. "Get out of here and take a cold shower. Let me handle the paperwork."

I growled. I didn't like the answer, but she was right. "Thanks."

I might need to stop talking smack about the vigilantes in the city. They might not have flashy powers, but they still put themselves at risk. Yet, here I was, a human matchstick, and I couldn't even take out a bunch of disgruntled hospital employees.

I bolted for the back of the hospital, faster than should have been possible. I needed to change and get back to Lei before she realized I was missing. Then I needed to contact Aiden. One fight with a villain and already my life had gotten complicated.

9

I HADN'T NEEDED A HOT SHOWER LIKE THAT IN YEARS. SCRUBS might seem like a practical solution when you're working with bodily fluids. However, within minutes, you realize why you don't want to see everything that gets on your uniform. I would not get out until the scalding water turned lukewarm. Most likely I'd take another before bed. I didn't want to find out what would happen if Smoke's blast of stupid left residue. Ew.

The Leos had shut down the hospital emergency room. The rest of the day, Lei and I shuttled patients from one hospital to the next. It was another day at the job, except for the first patient. Her orbital socket had been crushed and her jaw dislodged. Her face had already swollen, and the purple bruises were fast to fill in around the poor woman's eye. Before we took her vitals, I knew everything that was wrong. I should, because I was the one who did it.

I pushed the guilt aside, thinking about the phone charging on the couch. By the time I finished washing away the filth, I'd be able to text Aiden and make sure he had gotten away without a scratch. I had stared at the charger for five minutes before I swore. I couldn't will the stupid piece of plastic to power up any faster. At least the shower distracted me long enough for the damned thing to turn on.

"Speaking of turned on..." I couldn't help but smile at Aiden's insistence on this coffee date. I would gladly put some cream in his coffee if he allowed me. As the water cooled, I imagined him with me. It'd stay plenty hot. Two big guys in a tight space. There'd be no option but to be pressed up against him.

The soap had done its job of getting my skin clean, just not my mind. With a quick squeeze of my shaft, I decided I might as well take care of business. The cold water, however, meant I needed to find another place to get comfortable and unload.

Stepping out of the shower, I grabbed a towel, doing a light pat down. I walked out of the shower and tossed the towel on the couch, spreading it out so I could relax without leaving a wet spot on the fabric. A quick glance at the phone showed it had turned on, but was now working through a series of updates.

"You've got to be kidding me." Furiously clicking the screen did nothing to stop the manufacturer from hijacking the device. "Well, little buddy..." I plopped down on the couch, rolling back the foreskin on my cock. "It's your job to keep me busy now."

Yes, I regularly talked to my penis. With all the abuse I put him through, he'd earned a pep talk here and there. Besides, if I wasn't going to love him, who would? Well, if we could nail down a time, I hoped a certain journalist would.

He proved to be a persistent man, and I believed that would be the case when clothes came off. He'd have a hand on my chest, pushing me onto the couch, pushing my knees apart so he could get on his knees. It had been a while since a playmate came knocking, and there was no doubt my cock would be hard, eagerly awaiting the attention. By the time he pulled back my foreskin, there'd be a puddle of precum.

I closed my eyes while I played. As I wrapped my fingers around the base, giving it a firm squeeze, I imagined how much better it'd feel if it were him. After the events of today, thinking of Aiden handling my cock was exactly what I needed to take the edge off. Who needed superpowers? I needed a skilled mouth teasing the head of my cock before taking it all the way to the base. There were few things in life more satisfying than a hot guy determined to swallow the last inch. If they choked a little before they reached base, it'd be even hotter.

Running fingers along the underside of my shaft, I wanted it to be his tongue. When he reached the tip, would he lick the head or skip the foreplay and swallow it? Pulling back the foreskin, I opened my eyes to see I was already leaking. Would he take matters into his own hands, or would he want me to take charge? The thought of sliding my hand over the back of his head, easing him down, made my shaft rigid.

I coated my finger in precum, watching the thread of fluid between my finger and slit. I licked my finger, tasting a bit of the sweetness. I returned to massaging the head of my cock, letting the tingling reach my balls. There was no way I'd be able to hold back. By the time his mouth closed around my cock, I'd be bucking my hips, holding his head while I shot my load. I'd lie and say it was because of the sexy man, but it was more from nearly forgetting what it was like to be serviced.

What I lacked in duration, I'd make up in quantity.

"Take my cock," I mumbled. I'd hold the side of his head as I bucked my hips, nice and slow. It'd start with the entire length of my cock before I pulled out, giving him a chance to catch his breath. It wouldn't be long before the tempo picked up. If I didn't stop there, he'd be getting him a second mouthful in twenty minutes.

Either that or I'd stand up, pushing him down on the couch, ass in the air and—

The thought of my cock sliding down the crack of his beautifully round, hairy ass had my balls signaling the end of playtime. Reaching under my sack, I gave them a gentle tug, letting the warm sensation spread down my legs to pointed toes. The strokes turned quick, bunching the foreskin over the head, jerking it quickly.

I tried to slow my tempo, to ride the orgasmic wave. Every man tries, we really do, but impatience wins every time. With a final stroke, the flood doors opened and pleasure raced through every fiber of my being.

I cracked my eyes open to find my skin glowing. No, not in sexual bliss. The orange light pulsed as I gasped, choking back grunts. With the head of my cock peaking above the surplus of skin, the first shot of cum reached my chest, leaving a trail across my stomach.

It'd be better deep in Aiden's—

My body jerked in response to the thought. The growl renewed as the vein under my shaft throbbed, pleased at the thought of the thick man's ass. The second shot reached over my shoulder, hitting the couch with an audible smack. My torso was covered by the second and fourth strings of white. A shower was the only way to wash out a quality cum shot.

The sensation turned into a dull roar, vanishing far too quickly. While the orgasm subsided, the orange glow followed. Turning into a nightlight while railing a guy was going to make sex more interesting. At least my cock hadn't caught on fire. I might need more practice before I took this show on the road.

The phone dinged, then dinged some more. By the fifteenth notification, I reached to answer, but caught the sight of cum coating my hand. Reaching for the towel, I couldn't get at it without risking cum on the couch.

With a shrug, I licked it off my hand, surprised by its saltiness. A shot of protein never hurt anybody. It wasn't as hot post-orgasm, but as my cock twitched, it was enough to get my motor going again.

Convinced I got it all, I reached for the phone. With a swipe of my thumb, my heart sank. One after another, notifications appeared, warnings from the HeroApp™. The city was under siege as villains terrorized every corner of Vanguard. The app had moved to an alert warning citizens to stay inside at night.

"Jesus," I said. "I guess Griffin was right." I would never tell him that, but it appeared that heroes did keep the menaces of the city in check. I growled as I read a text Griffin sent hours earlier.

"Told you so." I would never hear the end of it.

Thankfully, the next message had a number I recognized. I deleted that punk Griffin and moved to Aiden's text.

A: Don't be a hero.

A: You okay?

A: Not funny. Cops are making us leave the hospital. Where are you?

A: If you're dead, I'll be pissed.

A: You're never going to get ass this way.

I snorted at the man's determination. He had gotten away safely and had no idea that I turned into a firefly. Revealing that I had joined the league of spandex to a journalist for a superhero magazine might make things complicated.

X: Phone got smashed. I'm alive. How are you?

I switched over to the HeroApp™ while waiting for his reply. On any given night, two or three minor villains popped up. But tonight, I lost count at twenty-two small crimes taking place and two major events underway. The city wasn't going to be safe, not until the heroes came back.

"Maybe..." I flexed my hand, forcing the knuckles to bulge on my right hand. I had driven my hand through a concrete wall without feeling pain. Somehow, I shot fire like a flamethrower. Somewhere inside my body was a leather suit waiting to make an appearance. "Don't want them, but maybe..."

The phone vibrated, and I picked it up, expecting to see a text. Instead, a photo from Aiden had come in. He was sitting in the bathtub with strategically placed bubbles. On the side sat a glass of bourbon, and I swear I could see an old-school boom box just out of focus in the frame. The message simply read, "Been worse."

X: Better if you weren't alone.

A: True. Did you see the new superhero in the hospital?

X: Lol. From my hiding spot? No.

A: He's the answer.

I wasn't sure where he might be going with this. I knew from listening to Griffin that heroes maintained secret identities to keep the people around them safe. If Smoke knew I was close with somebody, he could use it against me. Letting Aiden in on my little secret wouldn't end well.

X: To???

A: For the magazine. I'm going to land an interview with Blaze.

"Blaze?" I scoffed. "No. Not just no, but hell no."

A: He's probably out saving the city.

Saving the city, not so much. Pounding his fist against the face of bank robbers. Yeah, he might be up for that. I unplugged the phone and headed to the shower—again. Once I washed up, and got myself in a clean set of clothes, it was time to go out find some ass to kick.

10

THEY HAD BUILT VANGUARD CITY TO SHOW THE LIMITLESS potential of mankind. Sitting on the ledge of the Ward's tallest building, I understood the sentiment. Even while chaos ran rampant on the streets below, from here, I only saw man's determination to carve out a moment in history for themselves. It was unfortunate we also had a limitless ability for destruction.

A nearly full moon hung high in the sky, casting an eerie cool light across the city. Despite the ethereal glow, it didn't hide the blood coating my hands. There were splashes of crimson that still shimmered from the wetness.

From up here, the streets were quiet. I should quit, call it a night, and head home. Turning my hand into a fist, the blood pulled at the hair. I wanted more. The man attempting to rob a young woman received a matching pair of broken arms. The customer wielding a gun at the gas station would need a dentist after they wired his jaw shut. It had been an eventful night.

Touching the hole in yet another t-shirt, I thought about inching from the ledge. None of their punches hurt, neither did the gunshot, despite my flinching. If I dropped off an eight-story building, would I land without a scratch? If I was lucky, I'd land the classic pose, dropping to one knee with the pavement cracking underneath my weight.

What I wanted right now was to find Smoke. Smashing bandits was great fun, but it didn't stop the man who threatened Aiden. Just thinking about his words, my pulse quickened and I swear I could feel the fire in my veins.

"You're not going to jump, are you?"

In the corner of my vision, a young woman stood on the ledge. The signature purple costume gave away Hellcat. I couldn't help but note how quietly she moved. I'd have to put a collar with a bell on her. It couldn't be a coincidence that she found me hiding here.

"How did you find me?" The wind whipped through her ponytail, but she didn't turn to face me. Sliding hands into her pockets like a regular schmo, I couldn't believe she had been out saving the city this evening.

"Did you track me down?"

She grabbed a seat nearby, legs hanging over the ledge. A second later, she pulled off her black gloves, setting them to the side. The zipper from her collar slid down and she fanned herself. Despite getting comfortable, she didn't touch her mask. She might be willing to get cozy, but Hellcat didn't trust me, not yet. Thankfully, my suit shared the sentiment and maintained the cowl.

"I turned on a police scanner. Would you believe some idiot was going around beating the snot out of crooks? Instead of paying attention to where he was. Witnesses recorded him slugging a teenager."

"He had a knife."

Pulling out her phone, she flipped through the screens. Holding it up to my face, she put the video on display. "Supervillain beats teenager." I scoffed. They didn't have a clue what really happened. The kid was lucky I hadn't pulverized every bone in his hand.

"You're a rookie." She tucked the phone away. "We all start somewhere. But you're not making things easy for yourself."

"Since when is that a superhero's job?" The words sounded childish the moment I spoke them. I complained about the hero-worshipping titans running around and their lack of conscience. I should at least attempt to be better than them.

"Dial down the brutality. I've seen the video. You're obviously working through something, but the city isn't your shrink's office."

"It gets results."

A villain had triggered an alarm in a nearby bank.

While I appreciated Hellcat stopping by to give me a lecture, I had more work to do. Without a word, I pushed off. The whoosh of the air was almost unbearable. I let my limbs relax, preparing for the pavement.

"Booyah!" Down on one knee, the cracks rippled outward. I froze. I expected pain, a broken bone, or at least a dull ache cascading through my body. Nothing. Standing, I flexed the suit, stretching around my biceps. Power rippled along my skin, and I had to admit—I liked it.

The bank alarms rang. With the number of incidents taking place throughout the city, it could be hours before the cops reacted. Thankfully it was after operating hours and the streets were mostly clear. With the rise of villains in the city, people had gone into hiding when the sun set. They hoped waiting out another night of terror would cause a peaceful sunrise.

The robber didn't bother to wear a mask. Without heroes, the villains claimed the streets, no longer caring about the consequences of their actions. He must be my age, a slender man with enough face scruff that he'd be attractive if not for committing a felony. It'd be a quick save, slap him around, toss the money back in the bank and I'd add another notch to my belt.

Bang.

The first reaction of an amateur crook seemed to be shoot and ask questions later. I tried catching the bullet out of the air, scoring extra-cool points but it struck my chest. It signed the death warrant of another t-shirt, but the suit underneath absorbed the impact.

Speed. I wasn't as fast as the Zipper, not by a long shot, but a guy my size typically relied on brute strength. He fired twice. Why do they always shoot after seeing the first one did nothing? If you can't stop a man with one bullet, twenty more aren't going to make a difference.

Shoulder down, I hit the man in the torso, launching him into the glass doors of the bank. They cracked under his weight. If he was like the rest, the next stage of this fight would be him begging for me to let him go. It was like they all read the same playbook.

"I'm going to kill you."

Oh, that was a new twist to the evening. False bravado, I hadn't seen that one yet.

"Are you?" As he peeled himself from the glass, he balled his hands into fists. Seriously, I'd need to ask Griffin about this. If bullets didn't stop me, did he think his fists would fare any better? His reaction was almost ridiculous.

I let him get the first punch, landing it squarely against my stomach. There's no point in giving him hope that this would end any other way. Wrapping my hand around his throat, I lifted him into the air.

"Kill you," —he struggled to spit out the words— "then your family."

Smoke had made the same threat. The supervillain's words carried more weight than a desperate street thug.

But it gave away how quickly they'd turn to violence to get what they wanted.

The thug started to speak when I slammed him against the glass. Holding him off his feet, I could easily snap his neck and put an end to his miserable existence. I held his life in my hands, and with no effort, I could ensure he'd never commit another crime.

"He has a family."

Hellcat had gotten to the street faster than I expected. I don't know why she cared if the man had a family. What should it matter? He was a criminal that needed to be put down.

"You're making it up."

"His lanyard." She moved closer, pointing to the strip of white coming out of his jean pockets. Written in bold red letters: Vanguard Middle School.

"They'd be better off." My fingers tightened. "They don't need scum for a father."

"Life is precious. *All* life is precious." She moved closer; her feet barely made a sound on the pavement. "You don't get to decide who lives and dies. You're not the judge, jury, and executioner."

I had said those exact words a dozen times as I trained new paramedics. Whether the patient owned a million-dollar business or had been the one to plow his truck through a stoplight, they were the same. The man's body twitched and I pulled my hand away. He coughed, sucking in air.

We don't get to decide.

The guilt did more damage than the bullet. I scolded the superheroes for their lack of ethics, their constant need to put themselves above others. It had only been a day, and already I had turned into one of the egomaniacs.

The man scurried to his feet, running down the street, eyeing over his shoulder.

"Well," she started, "good job not killing him. But you didn't need to let a criminal get away."

Staring at my hands, I ran through the night, recounting the number of times I knocked the sense out of a criminal. I wanted to blame my anger, that it clouded my judgment, but it was more juvenile. Prometheus had entrusted me with a little power, and I abused it. Now came the anger.

"I'm just like them," I whispered.

"Welcome to the club." Hellcat patted me on the shoulder. "We all get caught up in the beginning. It's a rush."

"I could have killed him."

"Sure," she said, "but you didn't. It's a start."

A lick of flame rolled up my arm, igniting the sleeve of my t-shirt, burning the cotton. The fingers of the suit glowed, a first for the evening. I knew I could summon fire, or I thought I could, but despite my attempts, it hadn't come when I demanded it. Of course it appeared when I questioned my heart.

"Look..." Hellcat moved between me and the crushed doors. "You're the only powered person in the city. You might not be the hero we wanted, but you're all we've got."

"I'm not a hero." After nearly killing a middle school teacher, nothing about me felt heroic.

"Heroes aren't born," she said. "Get that comic crap out of your head. They're made. Do you think I woke up kicking ass and taking names?"

"Kind of," I mumbled.

"Well, yeah." Humble wasn't a word in Hellcat's dictionary. "But I lost my fair share of fights too. I was about to hang up my mask when a man offered to train me."

"You're offering to train me?"

"I drew the short straw at the vigilante meeting," she laughed. "I've been here before. So how about you take that pity party, clean up, and we find a more productive way for you to use that anger?"

In the ambulance, if I walked away from a call feeling I didn't do everything I could, I beat myself up for it. I'd read, ask questions, and the moment I had the chance, I'd prove I could be better. One day with powers and it was as if I had forgotten myself. I might be masked, but underneath the nifty alien costume, I was still Xander.

I nodded.

"Okay," she said. "First, I need a name. There is no way in hell I'm calling you Blaze. I have an image to uphold."

If I didn't know better, I'd assume the woman behind the mask took pep talk tips from Lei. Yet again, the women in my life were going to whip my ass into shape.

11

"YOU KNOW I CAN HURL FIRE, RIGHT?"

"Okay, big shot." Hellcat stepped back into the alley, motioning to the dumpster. For a hero without abilities, she wielded her sarcasm like a cosmic power. When I didn't summon it, she continued her prodding. "Well, show me these amazing abilities. I'm ready for shock and awe."

I had gone toe-to-toe with Shadow, hurling fire like a badass. This garbage-can had no idea the danger coming its way. I thrust my hands forward with a loud grunt. There was no warmth, no burning along my skin. Most of all, there was no pillar of fire obliterating the garbage.

"Invisible fire? That's a new power!" She squinted, and I could feel the mounting attitude. "Can you turn invisible when nobody's looking? The villains of Vanguard won't know what hit them."

"Tone it down. I still have that entire strength and bulletproof thing going for me."

I had barely extended my middle finger in her direction when she spun about. The heel of her shoe caught my chin. The momentum allowed her to hook her arm around my neck and swing her body to my back. I tried to turn, to drive my elbow into her mask, but she easily dodged the blow.

"Is clumsy a power?"

Her heel struck the back of my knee. Wrapping her arm around my neck, she held me in place with her leg. I couldn't gain leverage to grab her over my shoulder. I had power at my disposal, and I was being bested by a vigilante who knew how to kick.

Pointing a fist at the dumpster, I let loose a stream of obscenities. The fire gathered at my forearm, pulsing as it shot from my hand, slamming into the side of the bin. It rocketed upward, metal screeching along the side of the building.

Hellcat let go, backing away. "Until you can be consistent, it's best not to rely on your fireworks."

"But—"

"Me..." She moved where I could see her patting her chest. "Mentor. You..." She gestured in my direction. "Mentee. Listen, before I have to send you to detention."

I bit my tongue, a sign of a newly growing maturity. It was aggravating that I understood what she was saying. I didn't want to be a hero, but okay, I had a skill set that made me useful. Except, it only showed up sometimes. Hard to scare villains when you have to tell them to wait until I turned into a living matchstick.

"It'll be okay. The public thinks superheroes get their powers and overnight they're out saving the streets. That's why there are so many teams, and they go through members so quickly. Think of it like superhero boot camp."

"So you've done this before?"

Hellcat laughed. "God, no. But right now, seems I'm your best bet."

No powers, no experience, and yet, I couldn't see any other options. Prometheus had made a mistake in choosing me as his heir. Sure, getting shot and laughing it off was a fun parlor trick, but it didn't make me a hero. Hellcat had bested me with a couple of swift kicks.

"I'm—"

"Scared?"

"No."

"Determined?"

"Well—"

"You think this is all a mistake, and you should go home and call it quits?"

"I mean—"

With no fanfare, Hellcat ripped down the zipper of her leather jacket. In a dark alley, a vigilante flashed me. No, worse than that. She took my hand and placed it just above her bra. She held it there, making sure my fingertips grazed her skin.

"I took my first bullet at age twenty. It was me or a school kid." She dragged my hand to the side of her navel. "Metalica turned her fingers into blades and ran me through. But I wouldn't let her murder an innocent bystander."

The skin along her torso read like a fighter's version of brail. Pink scars were visible across almost every part of her body. Hellcat might be a skilled fighter, but even she couldn't win all the time. I moved to a square of gauze covered in red blotches.

"This?"

"Shadow," she growled. She stepped back, zipping up the jacket, returning to the indestructible Hellcat. "You can be fast, but you'll encounter somebody faster."

Before I could ask questions, she turned and walked toward the mouth of the alley. We had ventured to a questionable part of Southland, and it surprised me that we hadn't been mugged upon arriving. It seemed without the heroes, more than a few citizens had indulged in their criminal tendencies.

"Are you coming?"

I sulked, so sue me. I followed until she stopped me with an outstretched hand. She pointed to the ground, where the streetlight cast a shadow on the pavement. With another step, I'd leave the darkness and be visible to nearby citizens of Vanguard.

"Superheroes don't need to deal with this. For now, we're hiding in the shadows. It adds to our mystique."

"What other rules should I memorize?"

"Don't give monologues. That's for villains."

"Really?"

"Oh, and..."

She trailed off before kneeling in a crouch. The vigilante ground the toes of her boots, trying to gain better leverage. With one hand, she pointed at her eyes before gesturing toward the street. There were several dozen citizens walking along the sidewalks, but it was a hooded young man glancing over his shoulder that caught her attention.

"A kid?"

"A thief."

"You want me to stop a brat from stealing?"

"You want a lesson in being a hero? Sometimes the biggest victories are in the mundane. If you're—"

Nope, no more monologues. I stepped into the light, not to chase the teen, but to put distance between myself and Hellcat's rules. I had dealt with addicts determined to break into my ambulance. If she thought this was going to be a challenge, I'd scare the kid straight and be home in time for—

The sounds of the street vanished. The symphony of

car horns, squealing tires, or even scuffling feet evaporated. My ears hadn't failed. Even the deep bass of the subway turned off as if by a magical switch. When I caught the boy's face, his eyes glowed a vibrant green. I reconsidered listening to Hellcat's speech.

The kid inhaled, his chest rising. My brain attempted to seize control of my body and set me running in the opposite direction. They taught citizens from grade school to flee battles between heroes and villains. There had been seminars on how to not be used as a hostage. But I wasn't normal, not anymore. I was... Inferno—no, that sounded worse than Blaze.

While I debated superhero names, the kid pulled back his hoodie, revealing golden curls. Other than the eyes of doom, he looked like any other kid out after sundown committing petty crimes. The exhale wasn't a simple expelling of carbon dioxide, of course not. He screamed, an ear-piercing, blood-curdling—

The high-pitched tone turned a deep bass. I watched as the pavement of the road rippled, bits of rock flying in my direction. There wasn't time to react, not before it sent me hurtling into a building. Even from thirty feet, he hammered away with his powers, causing the brick to push inward, leaving a giant-sized "me" crater.

"Fuck. This." Even shouting, I couldn't hear myself.

I spotted Hellcat out of the corner of my eye. I thought she might swing in to karate chop the kid. She could have used one of those tranquilizer darts they always seemed to have. No, instead, she was holding a sandwich while she tried to open a can of soda one-handed. It was the wink at the end that did me in. Tough love, I got the message. I deserved nothing less.

Pushing off the wall, my limbs strained until I dropped to the sidewalk. I tried taking a step, but vertigo took over and I braced myself against a post office box. The kid's screaming stopped, his eyebrow raised as he processed. I tried willing the fire, summoning the pillar of flame. I shouldn't have wanted to turn him into ash, but after trying to pierce my eardrums, I'd at least crisp his edges.

Nothing.

"Dammit." My ears continued ringing.

Shaking my head, Hellcat came into view. Her lips were moving. I tried making out the words, but rolled my eyes when I discovered she was just taking another sip from the can. I needed a new mentor.

Okay, no fire. The suit remained intact. Eyeing the broken wall, any other person would have been pulverized into a fine powder. He might be a kid, but the brat needed to be taught a lesson in manners. The city's sounds vanished again while the kid made a show of sucking in the noise.

"Not today, Satan!"

Fingers pressed into the metal of a mailbox until they pierced the blue exterior. With a sharp jerk, it pulled from the cement. Seconds later, the mail receptacle soared through the air. I had never been one for athletics, and I doubt I could throw a baseball. But if hurling mailboxes became an Olympic sport, I'd earn a gold medal.

"Score." The mailbox hit the kid, bouncing him against a car. As he reached for the side-view mirror, I knew the fight wasn't over. I ran across the street and jumped as an angry driver honked his horn. At least my hearing wasn't completely shot, a small miracle.

I grabbed the kid by the shirt, slamming him against the car. The alarm went off before I kicked the fender hard enough that it pushed onto the curb. Who knew super strength could be this dangerous?

I struck his throat with the edge of my hand as he started to inhale. He grabbed at his neck, clawing at his skin, struggling to breathe. He might be a teenager, but if he could destroy a street and hurl me like a rag doll, I considered him dangerous. Punks like him made heroes a necessity, and I hated it. I hated *him*.

The heroes of Vanguard were self-aggrandizing assholes. Quite literally, they hovered over the city, above us, the people they swore to protect. Screeching boy made them a necessity. If we eradicated people like him, we wouldn't need defenders. But no, instead these psychos were deposited in prison and given the chance to return to the streets.

I drew back my fist, a warm light glowing across the

kid's face. This close, I could see the reflection in his eyes, a fiery ball of death, ready to break his nose before melting his skin. I eyed my fist, the fire nearly consuming my forearm and hand.

It'd only take a single punch. One.

I slapped the kid with my fireless hand. Shaking my matchstick limb, the ball of death vanished. I *could* have killed him. He might be a thieving banshee, but he was also somebody's baby boy. The rage pulsing outward turned inward, angry I had entertained the idea. When he objected, I struck him again and this time, he went limp.

I turned, ready to yell at Hellcat when I caught sight of a dozen citizens of Vanguard. Their faces hid behind cellphones and tablets as they recorded a successful confrontation. This is where a hero normally posed, signed a few autographs, and kissed a baby or two.

"Nothing to see here, folks."

"You have powers," a young woman claimed. "A hero with powers!"

"Are you sure he's not a villain?" A nearby man questioned her statement. When it came to heroes, regular Joe's should question their intentions. But right now, while holding a supervillain, I needed them to disperse.

I started to wave them off, but realized there was a better chance of herding cats.

Hellcat hadn't moved as she crushed the can before shooting it into a recycling bin. I understood where she acquired the name. Not the hell part, but the cat. She was as annoying as a sanctimonious feline. When the sirens grew loud enough to drown out the crowd, she signaled for us to vacate.

I set down the kid and pointed at the questioning man. "Make sure he doesn't get up."

I stormed toward the alley, elbowing through the growing crowd of superhero fans. There was something demoralizing about a superhero having to walk away. Could I really claim victory when it came to a slapping match with a kid? I'd probably be painted a schoolyard bully by the media, but knowing Vanguard, I'd have the key to the city by brunch.

"You'd be a lot more useful if you could fly."

"Yeah," I grumbled, "I'll get on that."

"You haven't said much since you nearly killed a toddler."

"Hush."

Hellcat had waited for hours to bring up the incident with the kid. Instead of giving me a 'good job, champ,' she'd led me through the city to the rooftop of a redbrick apartment building. I expected more fighting, or at least a chase here and there. Instead, she was the oddest dressed tour guide I had ever seen.

"What were you thinking about when it happened?"

"It?"

She gestured to her arm and made explosion sounds. When I didn't respond, she plopped herself down on the roof ledge. Swinging her feet sixty feet above the pavement below. I had to admit, the view of the city from this height was beautiful, even if I shared the moment with a lunatic.

"It's an involved story."

"Cliff Note's version."

"It would give away my identity."

She froze at the mention of my mundane life. Throughout the night, she checked her phone each time it vibrated. Making sure I couldn't read over her shoulder, she'd text somebody on the other end. As her heels stopped hitting the ledge, I had to wonder if the texts were related to Hellcat's alter ego.

"Never give away your identity. Once it's out, they'll come from you when you're not prepared."

"I'm always—"

"Or your loved ones."

Would a villain really travel a thousand miles to take my sister hostage? I pitied the fool who tried. She had more guns than ex-husbands. Once they realized she was going to wear the pants in the relationship, that had them packing. Villains weren't so different.

But then there were the guys. I bet Bernard could hold his own when boxing with another person, but powers? No,

I think he, Alejandro, and Griffin were prime supervillain hostage bait. Then there was the question of Aiden.

"Is that who you've been texting?"

She slapped her thigh and let out a laugh. "No. That's my work phone. The heroes of Vanguard are curious about a new man with abilities."

"Curious or suspicious?"

"Both," she admitted.

"You just casually text back and forth? Please tell me there's a group chat."

"No, it's a multi-multimillion dollar cellular network using direct satellite connections. It's a perk of having a few rich do-gooders around. Since the de-powering, they've helped mobilize the vigilantes."

"Wow," I said, "I didn't think this was that organized."

"I mean, we're basically a union at this point."

She spoke about the heroes as if they were the type of people you'd go out for cocktails with after a hard day at the office. I had assumed she was one of the discarded vigilantes who never got asked to join a team because of her lack of powers. It hadn't occurred to me that it might be a choice.

"Do they have any idea how they lost their powers?"

"Dr. Sincerbeaux believes somebody could do it with enough smarts."

"Tech?"

"Well, Dr. Arcane believes its magic."

"Nobody has a clue, do they?"

"None," she admitted.

For all their efforts and godlike abilities, they were helpless. Their frustration warmed the darkest parts of my heart. And yet, it was undeniable. Without them, crime was on the rise and the city was under siege. It pained me, but right now, Hellcat was the most knowledgeable person at my disposal.

"Can I ask you a serious question?"

"Shoot, cowboy."

"Why do you do it?"

I expected a fast reply with a sarcastic undertone, but all I got was a long pause. At first, I thought perhaps she hadn't heard, but from the corner of my eye, she stared at the city. What had I been thinking? We weren't close, and asking about the reasoning behind the heroics was—

"I needed a hero when I was a kid."

"There were more back then. Plenty for you to look up to."

"No," she replied. "Not role models. They shot my parents when a robbery went sideways. If there had been one, they could have protected my parents. Or maybe they could have gotten them to the hospital."

A paramedic worth their weight could have jumped in and saved the day. I'd have gladly taken that call to ensure they made it to the operating room alive.

"I needed a hero," she repeated. "Going out there is to

make sure there are fewer orphaned kids. It's how I make my parents proud."

I didn't have words. The mask on her face promised broken bones, lacerations, and more than a few concussions. But it gave her a sense of identity, hope, and purpose. I respected her motivation, even if I didn't agree with the outlet.

"And you?"

I held up my hands, inspecting the suit covering my skin. Prometheus had imbued me with power I still couldn't fathom. Even if I could access it and turn into a living fireball, did I want to use it? His dying wish had made my stance on superheroes extremely murky. But despite my disdain, I followed her to the top of this building.

"None of this is by choice."

"I don't mean the mask, medic."

Hellcat had seen my face without the mask. I shouldn't be surprised that she uncovered my secret identity. I assumed she knew, but we weren't going to talk about it like some sort of superhero code of conduct.

"Fixing broken things is my schtick." It was my go-to answer when people asked about my job.

"If you say so." She stood. Offering me a hand, she dragged me to my feet. "We're at the end of our night. I need to get back to my life."

"I should do the same."

"Or..." She smiled, making her appear far more sinister than it should. "You can ask me why I brought you here."

I assumed this building had a great vantage point. I couldn't imagine why she'd insisted on this rooftop.

"Why?"

"There's a journalist in apartment 7C I thought you'd be interested in seeing."

"Aiden?" She already knew my identity. There was no point in trying to hide my connection to him.

"You need to stop being selfish. We do this for reasons beyond ourselves. When you have somebody worth saving, you'll understand why we put on the masks."

Before I could answer, the woman jumped off the ledge. I peered downward as she somersaulted, and my muscles tensed as I prepared for a splat. But Hellcat lived up to her vigilante namesake. With an arm held out, something shot from under her jacket. Grappling onto a building, she sped downward until the line tightened. The woman looked like a modern-day Tarzan as she soared upward, covering blocks in a few seconds.

"Not fair," I mumbled. I think I'd rather take on a supervillain.

12

IT'D ONLY TAKE A KNOCK. INCHES SEPARATED MY KNUCKLES from connecting with the metal door. I saved innocents, foiled robbers... hell, I stopped bullets with my chest. But staring at the embossed 7C on Aiden's door, I feared I had met my match.

"Just knock." Even whispering the words caused my heart to beat a little faster. I wasn't there because he saved me, and no villain required heroic intervention. This was a simple emotion tying knots in my stomach. The conflict played out like a turbulent storm. One moment my brain retreated and my heart said, "I want this," and in the next, the script flipped. I wanted this, but did I deserve it?

Two knocks came from the other side of the door. I nearly jumped from the confident bang echoing through the hallway.

"In case you weren't sure how doors worked." Even muffled through the door, I imagined the words came with a sly grin. It should have calmed my nerves, but knowing Aiden was only inches away, the butterflies flapped with reckless abandon.

I knocked.

"Who's there?"

Was he really going to make me say it? I owed him my life, but groveling was not on the agenda. I scowled at the small eyehole, ready to give him a sarcastic remark. Betrayed by my body, my knuckles struck the door. Well, might as well go for broke and do it again.

The door opened and Aiden tried looking surprised. "Were you waiting long?" He could fight it, but the edge of his lip turned up. I didn't like that he held all the cards, but seeing him in a white undershirt and a pair of basketball shorts, he stole my breath.

"Xander..." his voice turned serious. "Are you okay?"

I wasn't okay. I was smitten.

"Uh, I wanted to see you." I could bury it underneath sexual innuendo and the thought of him straddling my hips. But the truth of the matter... it was that shit-eating grin that I wanted to see. I had never been an emotional man, but it was the truth. I wanted to see his stupid face.

"Here I am."

"You're going to make this awkward, aren't you?"

He nodded. "I'm enjoying this."

Despite surviving a shotgun blast, the playful banter from this handsome man nearly did me in. I spent the majority of my day nestled in the comfort of my rage, a general annoyance for the world. But here, with the man I daydreamed about, I could barely form words.

"I wanted to say thanks." I slid my hands in my pockets, trying to avoid being any more awkward than necessary. "You know, for saving my life." I dropped my eyes.

"You could have said that in a text."

Alejandro would be in stitches when he heard how the mere sight of Aiden evaporated my swagger. Even Griffin had more game than I did at that moment. I balled my hands into fists in my pockets, mustering the courage to put it all on the table.

In a graceful movement, his hand slid to my back and...

Aiden kissed me.

Rushed, his lips pressed against mine, his beard brushing against my chin. He lingered, and with my eyes closed, I could only sense the confidence. I could have shown up, dropped my pants and spent the night sweaty, but my heart spoke louder than my cock.

The kiss was soft, and too quickly, he pulled back. I leaned in, chasing one more second. The first move had been made, but I wouldn't let it be the last. I wanted—no, I needed whatever drug he pumped in my veins.

I caught his hand as he retreated. Stepping across the threshold, I had yet to sort where I wanted this to go. There were a thousand questions, and they quieted as I slid a hand to his neck, thumb grazing the edges of his facial hair. He held firm, letting me make the next move.

"I needed to see you," I whispered.

His forehead pressed against mine. "Still here." Smartass.

He tasted like cinnamon toast. This time, there was nothing chaste about the kiss. My hand slid to the back of his neck, pulling him tightly as I opened my mouth. He let me set the pace as my tongue touched the tip of his. The dams opened, and I realized what I wanted—a sexy man willing to let the butterflies flap their wings before he calmed them.

His fingers pulled at the loops in my jeans. Leaning back, he pulled me into the living room of his apartment. He never broke the kiss, letting me hold him firm, grazing his tongue along mine. Smacking the door, it slammed shut. I hadn't come with a plan, and standing in the man's apartment while I drank in his sexy was as far as my mind allowed me to think.

He broke the kiss, but didn't let go of my pants. His belly rested against my torso, giving me enough space that he wouldn't be aware of the bulge in my pants. Part of me wanted to throw him on the couch and peel the shirt off his body, but it'd mean breaking contact.

"Do you thank everybody like that?" Even though we were alone, the words came out in a whisper.

"Only the ones who save my life." This wasn't about bedding a sexy man and adding another notch to my bedpost.

"Good to know you have standards."

"They've been debated before."

He patted me on the side of the face, the grin returning to his face. "If you weren't so sexy, I'd slap you." On the second pat, I placed my hand over his, enjoying the warmth of his touch.

"I should go before I—"

"No."

The word hung in the air, a command. I was willing to go and be a gentleman. We could pick up over coffee, talking about that time I nearly died, or a supervillain tried to kill us. But as he bit his lower lip, I didn't want to be a gentleman.

"I was just about to take a shower."

"I wouldn't want to interrupt your—"

"Don't be a smart ass," he scolded.

"I didn't bring my bathing suit." It was my turn to taunt and tease.

"Good."

Dammit, he won this round.

Aiden's apartment wasn't large, but with most of the lights off, it was hard to tell. The front door opened into the living room that held a large couch and dining room table against one wall. Past an island, the space continued to the kitchen. On one side, there was a door to a bedroom, and he took me by the hand, guiding me into his personal space.

The master bath was larger than necessary. He stepped in, and a second later the hiss of water filled the silence. When he returned, the light from the bathroom left him in a dark silhouette. If I wasn't going to throw him onto the bed, I didn't quite know the etiquette for a first-time shower where we weren't washing cum off one another.

The shower was a large stall, surrounded by ceramic tile, and big enough to fit a small party. The steam from the water made the air wet, and I looked forward to the sight of this huskular man dripping wet. I tried to pull at the button on his jeans, but found it rather stubborn. He reached for it, offering a helping hand, when I batted it away. "Nope, I've got this."

With a little more fidgeting, his jeans opened. Tugging at the zipper, I savored each click as it slid down. Before I could pull them off, his shorts slid from his waist, crumpling onto the floor. That's where pants belonged. I went to lift his shirt, and he stopped me from stripping him naked.

Every inch of my being wanted to lunge, to wrap my arms around him and feel his skin pressed against mine. Aiden bit his lower lip. This drop-dead gorgeous man's confidence broke as nerves took hold. I loved thicker men, the way their bodies curved and the soft padding that made them perfect for cuddling. But not every man saw those as positives. Something in my chest hurt as I worried Aiden might not...

My hands remained in place as I crouched down, resting on my knees. With the few inches of his belly exposed, I leaned in, kissing it gently. His fingers relaxed as I continued upward until my nose touched his shirt.

I slid my hands around his waist, pulling him close while I rested my head against his stomach. Aiden ran his hand over the stubble on my head. There were a thousand ways I could compliment him, trying to dismiss his fears, but nothing summarized my admiration.

Unbuckling my pants, I stood up. I leaned against the bathroom wall while I kicked them off. I stepped on the toes of my socks, tearing them off. The uncertainty remained, written across his face, questioning if he had made the right choice.

I couldn't say anything to erase a lifetime of the world telling him he should look one way or another. I stepped into the shower, letting the water drench my t-shirt and soak through my boxer briefs. His eyes widened and he let out a laugh.

"What are you doing?"

I took his hand and pulled him closer. He would either have to wave me off or step into the shower. The worry vanished as he laughed, stepping under the water. I wrapped my arms around his waist, leaning through the spray to kiss him.

"You're crazy."

I stepped back, leaning against the tile. The water had left his shirt see-through, and even his underwear turned transparent.

"What?"

"How'd I get this lucky?" He might think it was a rhetoric question, but I really wanted to know. My life had turned complicated, but the powers, the suit, all of it, none of it mattered with this beautiful man in front of me.

"You're going to give a guy a complex."

"Sir, if you could stop being sexy, I'll stop staring." It was my turn to smirk. "We both know that's a lie."

"You're not so bad yourself."

His eyes glanced down in a sly attempt to check my package. I took my chances, pulling my underwear down my legs, kicking them into the corner of the shower. If he didn't trust my words, my erection made it abundantly clear how turned on I was at that moment.

As the sheer white fabric of his underwear stretched outward, I couldn't resist. I stepped under the spray, putting a hand on the small of his back, pulling him tight. My free hand worked down the front of his briefs, cupping his package. The moment my hand touched his balls, he let out a gasp.

"It's been a while," he whispered.

"You're not the only one."

I moaned as his fingers circled the shaft of my cock. With a firm hand and quick stroke, I realized I could come in seconds. As the water poured down his forehead, coating the side of his face, I stole another kiss. There were no villains, no robbers, no responsibilities. Nothing in this shower mattered other than the softness of his lips.

"Aiden." His name was barely audible over the rushing water. "I want you."

He rested his forehead against mine and kissed my nose. "You have me."

"I want to—"

"Show me."

My cock throbbed. "You sure?"

He tightened his grip until I moaned again. "I'm yours."

I didn't need further invitation. The water hit him in the face as I spun him around. There were countless things I'd tell him were incredibly sexy, but one stood out above the rest. Sliding my hand into his briefs, I cupped his ass. This reporter had a backside that would make any man hard.

One hand held his hips while the other pushed between his shoulder blades. He leaned forward, bracing his hands against the wall. There were few things in the world more sexy than a thick man bent over, their ass screaming out its welcome.

I let my finger slide down the crack of his ass. His body was almost as hot as the water. I paused, letting my finger linger over that magic spot that caused him to push back. There are moments where the reality doesn't live up to the imagination. This was not one of them.

Pulling down the back of his underwear, the wet fabric framed his ass, writing an invitation I couldn't resist. I dropped to my knees, watching as the water funneled down his back. I ignored the deluge splashing against my face as I kissed his skin. His ass fit perfectly in my hand, and I gave it a firm squeeze, eliciting a gasp from the sexy man.

"I imagined this—"

"Me too," he interrupted.

There was only one reply. I buried my face in his ass, holding his hips like handles. There was a chance I'd drown as I ran my tongue down the length of his ass. Once again, I hit a spot that had Aiden pushing back. I greedily accepted his eagerness, burying my tongue. While I would have gladly spent an hour rimming the man, this was more of a utility slathering.

My hand followed the elastic of his waistband. Even through the water and drenched cotton, it was hard to ignore the impressive bulge he sported. Cupping his balls, I wrote him one last love letter with my tongue. Before I finished, he grabbed my hand, pulling it away.

"I won't last long." He squeezed my hand, lacing his fingers between mine. "Not if you..."

I rose, letting my cock nestled against his crack. Without letting go, I placed his trapped hand where it had been resting on the shower tile. With his ass pushed back, I leaned over his body, and thankfully, I was tall enough to kiss the back of his neck. He reached back, grabbing my hips, pulling me into him.

"Not if I, what?"

"I won't last if you fuck me."

"That makes two of us," I admitted. Perhaps if I had been fucking regularly, or if I had jerked off before knocking on his door. But as it stood, I'd be lucky if I got my cock in him before I fought off an orgasm.

Spit. He coated his fingers in spit before reaching back and slathering it on his ass. Oh well, this just reached another level of hot. Lube might make everything slide more easily, but spit brings out the primal nature of a top. The moment I knew he was coated in saliva, I wanted to bury my cock in this sexy man.

Holding my shaft, I swiped it up and down the crack of his ass, making sure I was as lubed as could be. Thankfully, I had been leaking precum since I arrived. I wasn't the biggest cock out there, but it was hardly a beginner model.

There was hard, and then there was I'm-about-to-fuck-a-sexy-bear hard. Even I was impressed by the stiffness of my cock. Lining up, I prepared to take my time easing into

Aiden, reading his body language as he moaned and groaned. But it was me who gasped when he pushed back, forcing the head of my cock into him.

"Damn." The word came out in a growl loud enough that his neighbors would start banging on the walls. He froze, holding still, and I feared his libido had written a check his ass couldn't cash. But with a slow rocking motion, he eased his way back.

"Jesus," he gasped, "you're huge."

I appreciated his gusto, but the last thing I wanted to do was hurt him. I withdrew, or at least tried. He moaned before reaching back and holding my hip.

"Slow." I think he meant the word for him more than me.

I wrapped him in a bear hug from behind. Leaning across his back, I let my stubble drag across his skin. Standing with him in the shower was already more than I expected tonight. I wanted to fuck him, but I *needed* his body pressed against mine. Everything had gone to shit, but as I held him, I hugged 'normal.'

The gasp brought me back to reality. I melted, holding him tighter as he slid down the length of my shaft. Okay, perhaps I lied, and *this* was what I needed.

"Gentle." This time, he turned his head to ensure I listened to the plea.

I didn't speak as I pulled out an inch before rocking back. The motion repeated, and each time he let out a content sigh. Any top worth his weight translates every cue and adjusted. But when Aiden's body relaxed, curving against mine, he went from gentle and slow to eager and determined.

Aiden shoved back forcefully, taking my cock to the hilt. He rode like a seasoned cowboy. I took control, holding his hips and sliding the length of my shaft from him before pulling him back to the base. If I had been in complete control, I could have set the tempo and made this a marathon instead of a sprint. But he had other plans.

The muscles along my calves stiffened, my body tensing, relaxing, and tensing again. At the beginning of every orgasm, the brain is hyper-focused. The cock is the only thing that matters, but the closer to orgasm, the sensation spreads outward. I tried to hold off, to ride the sensation, but then I heard my balls slap against his ass and willpower be damned.

"Come for me." The words were breathy, but it didn't diminish the command. I'd gladly fulfill his request.

Gripping his hips, it was two more strokes before I couldn't hold back. Holding him in place, my cock swelled, causing him to moan. Wrapping an arm around his chest, I pulled him upright, savoring the feeling of his wet skin against mine.

I let out a yelp as he dismounted. He turned, with a hand on his cock, and I recognized the parted lips and eyes peering downward. It was hot to think I had cum in this sexy man, but it'd only be complete if I returned the favor. Dropping to my knees, I held his cock in my hand. What he lacked in length he made up for in girth. I nearly whistled at the fact my fingers barely circled the shaft. I was determined, and swallowed him to the base.

"Fuck," he groaned.

He held my head in place, not needing any stimulation. Touching the back of my throat, I couldn't taste the cum, but it was more about not letting it go to waste. He gave one last thrust of his hips before pulling out.

Getting off my knees, I stood, staring at him while his chest rose and fell in quick succession.

"I just stopped by to say thanks for saving me."

He laughed, holding my neck. Leaning back, his body shook, the joyous sound filling the shower. He gave my cheek a pat before leaning forward. I thought the affair was about to end in a kiss when he stopped short.

"For saving your life..." The grin spread, infectious, until I had a stupid smile stretched on my face. "Best reload fast. A life is worth at least two or three rounds."

Tonight? If I had any insecurities when I first knocked at his door, my growing erection didn't notice.

13

G: BREAKFAST OR I STAB YOU.

X: Whoa. You sound like me.

G: Bernard is extra moody lately. I can't deal.

B: I'm in this chat.

A: Griffin's not wrong.

B: I hate you all.

X: I'll be there.

B: Don't be late.

B: I'll need an alibi when I kill them.

B: Just kidding.

B: Not kidding.

Now was the part of the conversation when everybody descended into lewd emojis and archaic memes. For a group of grown men, we acted like a bunch of children. We should be ashamed, but we'd be loud about it until the entire coffee shop stopped and stared.

Setting my phone aside, I laid back in bed, staring at the ceiling. It had been a long time since I stayed the night after sex. I found the ritual awkward. Aiden had attempted to exit without waking me, which was sweet, but now I didn't know if I should stay naked in bed, get up and make some coffee, or hunt down any juicy dirt I could uncover?

Coffee. I don't know why I even considered other options.

I scoured the bed for my underwear. I needed to do a better job of remembering where I disrobed. Nothing. Peeling back the cover, I was about to give up hope when I dropped to the floor, hunting for my boxer briefs.

"Where the hell—"

There are certain sensations the skin can recall just by thinking about it; a warm towel, a light touch, even the warm sands between the toes. The cool, wet slime worked its way along my arms. Quickly, it caused my gag reflex to kick in. Oh my God, it was awful. There was no controlling it, willing it underneath my skin. Seconds later, it had responded to the dilemma of being naked.

"Not now." It acted like fabric, pulling away from my body as I tugged at the collar. Despite stretching, it refused to tear. If I peeled myself out of it, would it vanish? Was it alive? While I was playing hero, I didn't care how it worked, just that it lets me be super. Now, I needed it to go away before Aiden discovered he had blown a superhero this morning.

"Did you say something?" The shower shut off. I kicked the door, slamming it harder than I intended. He probably thought I was going through his drawers, which would be easier to explain than wearing skintight latex.

"I don't need you right now." It's hard to make a whisper sound stern, but I tried my damndest. I found my t-shirt wrapped up in the sheets and tossed it over my head. Shaking out the linens, I was out of luck. I was about to give up hope when I saw the pile of damp clothes. I found underwear, socks, but still no pants. Without wasting a second, I pulled on the underwear. Damp, this was going to be a rough morning of chaffing. I ignored the fact they were inside out. Next, the socks.

I looked like a superhero on laundry day.

"Go away."

"Xander?" I pinned my foot at the base of the door. It held fast as Aiden attempted to open it. "Is everything okay?"

I looked down, grasping at how I'd explain the suit. Skin. Bright white thighs vanished into a pair of black briefs. Without so much as slither, the suit vanished. Thank you, an awkward conversation avoided.

"Sorry about that. Was hunting for my pants." I lied, sue me. "Much as I'd like to stay naked with you—" I had to pause and soak in the sight of him. Upright, I admired the curves of his body. He might be even sexier.

"Oh," he said, "yeah, I should probably get some work done."

Taking his hand, I placed it on my shoulder as I stepped in closer. "Trust me, I would much rather be right here."

"Still on for coffee?" The poor guy was worried that this was a one-night stand. I had done that in the past before, but now... yeah, it wouldn't be the last time. After a night of mind-altering sex, I was already thinking of what might happen next time.

Kissing him remained as amazing as last night. I broke away before the urge to throw him on the bed returned. "I'm expecting it."

"Pants are on the table."

"Stealing my clothes?"

"How else would I fashion a pillow boyfriend to sleep with?"

I gave him a pat on the ass as I walked into the kitchen. He vanished into the bedroom, opening and closing drawers as I slid on my pants. Scattered across the table were notes on legal pads of paper. There were several news articles torn from the paper.

"Powered hero saves hospital." I pushed it to the side, looking at the other clippings. "Vigilante demonstrates abilities." Even as I whispered the words, I couldn't fathom that my antics had landed me in several newspapers.

It was the last article that made me cringe. "Newest villain wages war." As I picked up the cut-out piece of paper, I unfolded it to see an image at the top. It was blurry and impossible to identify the hero. Karma never worked in my favor. I was glad to see at least my identity was safe.

"New Powers: Villain by Default."

I was about to ask Aiden which hack wrote the articles. I'd go down there, and before I finished, I'd burn down his office and beat the snot out of him.

On another paper, Aiden had written, *Who is Blaze?*

"Found my ticket, huh?"

"Ticket?" I didn't get his meaning.

"To becoming a staff writer."

I forgot he wasn't officially a reporter at Revelations. The work on the table bordered on a conspiracy theory. The only thing missing was a blue string linking it all back to a single mastermind. I set down the paper, trying to maintain a neutral tone.

"Why Blaze?" I nearly wretched saying the name.

Aiden started pushing paper about the table. He unfolded an article, pulled another from beneath the legal pad, and dropped a couple dozen photos from the HeroApp™.

"I'm going to get the scoop on Blaze." I needed a new name before this stuck. "There were a dozen accounts from the hospital. Then, a bank robber from a heist said he shot a man in the chest and he hardly flinched."

"Villains still have their powers, so what?"

"Blaze saved those people. Xander, he's not a villain. He's a hero, a hero with *powers*." The tone in his voice shifted, and it became obvious he was less talking to me and more reaffirming his own theory.

"Take it from somebody who chases heroes for a job. This is going to put you in danger."

"If I can get an interview with him or find out his origin, it would make my career. The people at Revelations will have to take me seriously. This is the story that starts my career."

Of course, I could put the suit on and sit down and have an interview with him. But I didn't want the spotlight focused on me. If I had stopped to read a newspaper, I'd have seen Blaze—God, that's a stupid name—was already getting more attention than I wanted. Half the city already believed I was just another villain cashing in on the mayhem.

"It's about the truth," he said.

"Huh?"

"When I was a kid, I was enamored by the news. Here were a couple of people sitting behind a desk telling us all the information going on in the world. Two people. They shaped the opinions of tens of thousands of people. That's a lot of power. It's like a superpower in its own right."

I was worried Aiden was about to start a maniacal laugh. At any moment, he'd tear away his clothes to reveal spandex and a cape and declare his intent to take over the world. Was I standing at ground zero for a villain in the making?

"I don't want to shape opinions. There are too many people out there trying to do that. The world should see an unbiased truth. I don't think Blaze is the villain they're saying."

He looked at the paper sitting in the middle of the table. It held a single question, the source of the article and Aiden's driving force. Who is Blaze? It was touching that in a world where headlines were nothing more than clickbait, he wanted to enlighten the people. If it had been any other hero, I would have patted him on the back and asked what I could do to help.

"Heroes can't do it alone," he whispered.

I wanted to argue that the self-entitled jerks destroying our city for their own egos needed nothing from us. I wanted to launch into the same speech I gave Griffin every few days. Then I thought of Hellcat going out of her way and asking for nothing in return. Even Aiden, determined to shine a chivalrous light on a hero, wanted to help.

"Maybe you're right."

Even with Vanguard falling apart, the HideOut seemed unscathed. Patrons placed their orders and exited with large cups of coffee like it was any other day of the week. It was impossible to tell that we were slowly being overrun by criminals, or that at any moment an alien invasion could level the city.

Chad set the silver thermos on the counter, a routine that had become second nature. I chomped through my bagel as he turned away when he froze and eyed the canister. If things were normal, Zipper's sonic boom would rattle the windows as he swapped it out with an empty one from the previous day. Instead, Chad took the thermos and set it behind the counter, a defeated look passing over his face before he stapled on a smile and greeted the next patron.

"Do you think they're coming back?"

Griffin's question snapped me back to the trio at the table. While the world continued on as if nothing was happening, Griffin, Alejandro, and Bernard acted as if somebody had ran over their pet poodles. I could understand Alejandro's dismay, without superpowered people in his club tips must be pretty bad. It also didn't help that he probably hadn't been tossed around the bedroom since the depowering.

Between bites, I answered, "I don't know."

"No."

The entire table turned to Bernard. The man served as our anchor, the sound of reason as I threatened to kill people, Griffin acted aloof, or Alejandro turned into a nympho. Like me, his job depended on the superhero community, but where I could fall back on being a run-of-the-mill paramedic, his entire field focused on heroes. It couldn't be easy.

"Maybe?" It was the best I could afford him.

"I hope so," Alejandro chewed through his toast like it was one of his men. "I can't remember the last time I got laid."

"You could have sex with normal men?"

He gasped as if I insulted his mother. "Once you've had a gang bang with the Duplicator, you can never go back."

"Is he the one who makes clones?"

Griffin rolled his eyes as if I had made a fool of myself. "You're thinking of the Multiplier."

"Wait, I thought the Multiplier was the guy who could grow body parts?" Apparently, I needed to buy myself some superhero flash cards.

"That's Magnifier," Bernard said. "Griffin is judging you."

I eyed Griffin, his eyes burning a hole through my head. There were a lot of things I was good at. I could intubate a patient blindfolded. There wasn't a vein capable of hiding from my needle. I also knew every household agent to get rid of bodily fluids. However, I was willing to concede, nobody knew heroes better than Griffin. There was a temptation to ask him questions, to jeopardize my alter ego, to access some of his wisdom.

"I finally thanked Aiden." I decided to avoid sharing my secret identity.

"With your penis?" Alejandro dropped his toast. Pushing the plate aside, he rested his elbows on the table, leaning forward. "I want details."

"Not like that." Yes, just like that. I'm sure my cheeks were turning red, revealing my lie.

"Liar," Bernard said as he took a swig of coffee.

"I mean—"

"Don't you even think about lying?" I'm certain Bernard didn't stop drinking while he spoke.

"The man saved my life. I went to tell him I appreciated it."

"With. Your. Penis."

Alejandro dodged a sugar packet I tossed at his head. "I thanked him." I shoved a piece of bagel in my mouth. "Wifmahpeenas." Coy wasn't part of my playbook. But with the three of them staring, I suddenly felt the need to hide. I prayed the Sentient Squid returned and laid waste to the coffee shop.

"¡Es todo, cabrón!." Alejandro held up his hand as if he deserved a high-five. More than once, we had shared a celebration over a conquest, but this time it didn't seem appropriate.

"Wait," Griffin jumped in. "You stayed the night?"

Bernard set down his coffee cup, shaking his head.

"Griffin, it wasn't so long ago you had that look on your face."

"You mean..." Griffin leaned back in his chair. The newest member of the breakfast club slowly nodded his head. I was about to reach for the underside of the table and flip it.

"You have feelings for Aiden."

"Feeling in his pants," Alejandro said. He was prepared to throw up a hand for another high-five, but paused. "None of you are any fun."

"Let's not make it a thing," I begged.

"It's already a thing," Griffin replied.

"It's not."

Bernard raised an eyebrow. "You're acting like it's a thing."

"He has a thing," Griffin added.

"I hate you both."

Bernard's hand slid under the table, resting on my bouncing leg. He gave it a squeeze. "Eventually you'll admit it."

I had plenty of things to hide right now, but my encounter with Aiden wasn't one of them. Long ago, I had forbidden them from discussing my relationships over breakfast. No matter how many times I threatened to punch them, they persisted.

I balled my fists on the table. "There's nothing to admit."

"This is a reason to celebrate. Chad," Alejandro yelled at the owner, "a round of coffee for my companions. We're celebrating."

The barista was usually the first to nose his way into the conversation. Sweet and overly concerned with his patrons, Chad had a way of being disarming, funny, and uplifting in everything he did. However, as he walked over with a pot of coffee, he poured without commentary. His lack of input bordered on supernatural.

"Chad..." I reached out, tugging on his arm. "Are you okay?"

"Yeah, everything is fine." Fine. The word used by those who felt anything but. I had to wonder if his usual peppiness was a superpower, and now he functioned like the rest of us. While he tended to be a bit more than I could handle, the morose body snatcher was not an improvement.

"I, for one, am happy Xander found somebody." Griffin poured creamer into his coffee, ruining the cup as it turned a khaki color. "I thought at any moment he was going to be court-ordered into anger management."

My fist smacked the table, rattling the silverware enough that a momentary hush passed through the Hide-Out. I wanted to be angry with Griffin. It wasn't news that I had an issue with my temper. I spent years drifting from one employer to another, unable to "knuckle under." But as nails dug into my palm, I was angrier that the joking came with an air of truth.

"I didn't mean—"

"You did," I said.

Our dynamic had shifted. Without Bernard to mediate our extremes, we were teetering on a total friendship collapse. Unlike my younger self, I knew when it was time to remove myself from a situation. Sure, it wasn't the best coping mechanism, but it kept me from lashing out verbally, or worse.

"I have to head to work." I tossed a twenty on the table as I pushed my chair back.

"Tomorrow?" Griffin asked. It was a peace offering, a sign that I wouldn't let this drag me away from the others.

"We'll see." I'm sure it sounded petty, but it was the best I could promise myself. If I had given in to anger, I'd have flipped the table, given them each the finger and stormed off. I could control it. I *had* to control it. What worried me most—a part of me didn't want to.

"Wait, papi." Alejandro put money on the table. "I need arm candy and you're going my way."

Great, just great.

We had walked nearly three blocks through the Ward. We passed red brick storefronts holding quaint mom-and-pop shops, one of the charming aspects of this part of Vanguard City. Alejandro's loft was another block away, marking the midpoint between the HideOut and the ambulance bay. In the years I had known Alejandro, he had never gone this long without talking. His silence had grown more unnerving than his frequent rattlings.

"I can't take it anymore. This is the longest you've ever been silent. What is going on?"

He linked his arm through mine. On an evening out, it might be a romantic gesture. Two burly men, however, sauntering down the sidewalk made walking incredibly awkward. Thankfully, I found just about everything about our friendship lacking grace.

"You mean, me acting out of character is freaking you out? You don't say. The irony is—"

"Did you just keep your mouth shut for four blocks to make a point?"

"I died a little on the inside."

I stopped walking, jerking his arm so that he stopped. He raised an eyebrow, waiting for me to launch into a monologue. All I could do was laugh. It had been years since I met Alejandro, and I thought the man's weakness was silence. If left to his own devices, he'd ramble on for hours. Tears formed in the corner of my eyes as I struggled to catch my breath.

"Bernard is acting weird. Griffin went an entire meal

without mentioning comics. And you,"—he poked me in the chest— "you're being the weirdest of all."

"How am I being weird? Because of Aiden?"

"Xander, I've never lied to you." The others might dance around a topic, but Alejandro had a knack for cutting right to the chase. I had watched him tend bar, and he could charm the pants off even the noblest of heroes, but he never needed a silver tongue. "Let me be blunt. You have anger issues."

"Thanks." I rolled my eyes. "You're not the first—"

"Papi." He put a hand on my chest and stepped within my bubble. We were close, *very* close. The proximity had me holding my tongue. "I'm not sure if it's work or if something else is going on in your life, but it reminds me of the Xander I first met."

Years ago, Alejandro had been standing at the bar trying to get himself another gin and tonic. Two guys decided they wouldn't take no for an answer. He had been polite when he refuted their advances, but I had broken a nose, arm, and half a dozen fingers when they didn't take the hint. If it hadn't been for Alejandro dragging me off them, I'd have crushed one of their skulls with a bar stool.

"Ouch." That hurt more than I cared to admit. Here I thought I had been making progress.

"Bernard is the dad of the group. Griffin is our baby brother. Xander, you're the overprotective big brother. You don't get mad at us. You *never* get mad at us."

"It's happened before."

"Tell me when. I'll wait."

"I..." I sorted through the numerous times Bernard had to talk me down. I might have threatened to kill Griffin's boss, Alejandro's co-workers, and basically every man who broke up with any of them. "Well, damn."

"I thought therapy was doing you some good."

"Wait." I had never told any of them about seeing a therapist. Granted, I had only gone a half dozen times before I decided reliving my childhood was counterproductive. "How did you know about that?"

"I have my ways."

"Thank God you're cute."

"I do every day."

"Take care of yourself, handsome. I rather like my big brother willing to defend my honor. But let it be for a good reason and not because you're a giant man-child having a tantrum."

Speechless. Nearly. "Wait, who are you in this dysfunctional family?"

"The sexy middle child."

He patted me on the cheek before sliding his arm through mine again. Apparently, we had moved past the pep talk portion of the morning.

"Tell me about Aiden."

"It's not a thing," I repeated myself, hoping it'd sink in.

"Somebody protests too much. Stop being a jerk and tell me about him."

"He has a knack for being in the wrong place at the right time."

"So you two have that in common."

"He works at Revelations with Griffin's boyfriend. I'm not sure what he does right now, but he thinks he blew his chance at being a reporter. He's trying to make a name for himself."

"Ambition? So far, it sounds good."

"He has this naïve belief that he can make a difference by reporting the truth. Can you believe it? When has the truth done the world any good?"

"'Cause lying is such a noble pursuit."

"That's not what I mean."

We stopped in front of Alejandro's building. This part of the Ward had a smattering of old mills that had been converted into industrial-style apartments. It served as Alejandro's base of operation, or his den of sin, depending on who you asked.

"I need you to close your eyes."

Eyes narrowed, brows scrunched, and a sour expression tugged at my lips. I was about to protest, expecting him to slap me across the face. It took a moment before I remembered being shot and the lack of bullet holes in my skin. Suddenly, nothing Alejandro could manage seemed to be worrisome.

"Do it, scaredy-cat."

I closed my eyes. *Do your worse, Alejandro. I'm ready for you.*

"I want you to imagine Aiden the last time you said goodbye."

"What are—"

"Do it!"

The long, exasperated sigh made it clear what I thought of his exercise. But I played along. Aiden had slipped into a t-shirt and a pair of loose-fitting boxers. They had never been my favorite, but seeing the curve of his ass in them, I'd have to reconsider my bias. While his lower half was memorable, it was the way his eyes darted back and forth as he debated how our encounter was going to end.

I answered his insecurity with tenderness. One hand caressed his cheek while the other pulled at his waist. With only inches between us, I wanted to fill him...with confidence. It wasn't until he leaned forward, his forehead resting against mine, that I realized my own insecurities might have found their way to the surface. I already plotted a reason to return and stand with my knuckles hovering over his door.

The last words I said before kissing him goodbye were, "Next time, I'll bring my bathing suit."

"Xander." Alejandro poked me in the forehead. "Earth to Xander."

"Sorry." Nope, not even a little sorry.

"It's unsettling to see a smile on your face."

"I smile." Okay, the last time I remembered smiling this much was when Bernard accidentally poured salt in his coffee. I didn't dare laugh out loud at his plight, but I couldn't hide the grin.

"Nobody is getting hurt and you're smiling." I needed to find new friends. "I don't know what Aiden did to you. But every time you say his name…"

If ever I regretted opening my mouth, it'd be with the next three words. "I like him."

Alejandro patted me on the cheek. "Now that you've admitted what the rest of us already knew, we can get on with our lives."

"Jerk."

"It's a curse always being right."

I liked Aiden. If anybody else made the same statement, we'd all have nodded and returned to the previous conversation. Hell, Alejandro fell in love at least twice a week. But me? There were booty calls I enjoyed having a casual relationship with, but I didn't treat them like my little spoon.

"You're doing it again."

I growled. It was one thing to have an epiphany about wanting to see Aiden again, even if he was clothed. It was another to have somebody policing the expressions on my face. I'd have to practice in the mirror so I could dodge Alejandro.

"Before I go…" He let the words trail off, his attempt at

being coy. It was only a matter of time before he transformed from the caring friend back into his usual sex fiend self.

"I'm not telling you about the sex."

"That good?"

I couldn't hide the grin if I tried. "Yeah." Even as my body recalled the feeling of Aiden under me, my cheeks warmed. "It was very good."

"Is it going to be good again?"

Sly, Alejandro, very sly.

14

Lei swung the wheel before slamming the brakes. The ambulance swung about. She dodged the convertible, but we lost the driver's side mirror to a dump truck. I clutched the "oh, shit" handle tight, praying that my stomach caught up. Before I could take a steadying breath, the engine roared to life as she slammed the gas again.

"Hostiles on-site. Leos have arrived."

The dispatcher had named the three villains that stormed the power plant. Tank. Crete. Bulldozer. I considered all three bruisers—stronger than smart. Any of them could demolish a building without effort, but together, local law enforcement didn't stand a chance. The time where they'd wait for heroes to come and save the day had long since passed. Lei and I wouldn't be there to treat people with powers. We'd be working to keep regular folks from dying.

Two police cars turned onto the street ahead of us. They weren't doing nearly as well as Lei as they jumped the curb, trying to avoid hitting an oncoming car. While the police attempted to stop the unstoppable, I wondered if the vigilantes were going to arrive and pick up the slack. Even Hellcat's expert fighting wouldn't protect her against these brutes. If they landed a single blow, she'd be dead before hitting the ground.

"Look up," Lei said, pointing to the sky.

The streak of exhaust in the air reminded me of an airplane. But it wasn't nearly as big, and it looked like...

"Is that a man?"

"I think so." She pointed to the right. "There are two more. Villains? Or do you think..."

I wanted to believe the heroes had returned. It was an odd statement to think. Apparently, my opinions had shifted.

Lei pushed the gas pedal until it thudded against the floor. Our girl could hit seventy-five on a straight patch of road, but between the swerving from danger and skidding around corners, she only managed a meager sixty miles per hour. Lei and I normally swapped off driving detail, but after this, I'd gladly admit she was the better driver. Now, if only we survived her transformation into Mad Max.

"Holy shit." It was an understatement. Cop cars hung

from second-story windows. Our dedicated police force backed away from the ring of destruction created by the trio of villains. But as Lei let up off the gas, slowly rolling toward the action, help had arrived.

"Who are they?" Lei asked.

Whipping out my cell phone, I punched the HeroApp™ icon. Nearby viewers were already snapping photos. A warning flashed across the screen, listing the villains with a link to read more about their history. A green exclamation mark identified the arrival of three metallic heroes.

"Machinist. He's not a super." I scrolled through the details. "Blah, blah, blah. He's in one of those suits of armor, but artificial intelligence controls the others."

"Never heard of him."

"Logan Steele."

"The billionaire?"

"Yup."

Lei's eyebrow raised. "If I had a billion dollars, let's be clear, I'd buy myself a yacht. There'd be none of this building suits of armor and living out some midlife crisis."

She had a point. But thankfully, this billionaire had used his wealth to help protect the city. Was this the man that Hellcat mentioned? Between his bank account and proclivity toward tech, it'd make sense. While he traded blows with the villains, it was time for Lei and me to earn our paycheck.

"Ready?"

She shook her head. "No." Opening the door, she hopped out of the ambulance. "But when has that ever stopped me?" Into danger we went, the very core of what we did for a living. It was time to save the citizens of Vanguard.

Police officers running away from danger didn't bode well. The few still hovering on the edge of the circle were split between firing their guns at the villains and pulling their fallen brethren out of harm's way. Their ranks had been decimated, and now they relied on their last resort, bullets.

I eyed the rooftops, hoping I'd see the telltale shadow of a vigilante avoiding attention from the cops. There was nothing out of the ordinary, and I had to wonder if perhaps this was beyond their pay scale. If the Centurions were available, this fight would have been over before it started, but right now it seemed like it was up to the humans to defend the city. Humans and me, that is.

"Are you coming?"

From twenty feet away, Lei's shouting could barely be heard over the sound of screeching metal. She had gotten close to an overturned car. It wasn't on fire, but with how the underside curved, it would be deemed a loss. Lei was already on the ground, taking the vitals of an unconscious police officer. As I got closer, she pointed to another downed man, this one with a wound in his shoulder.

"Get him." I ignored her take-charge attitude. If it kept

people alive, I'd gladly take the backseat. Bullet hole, not exactly a walk in the park, but at least the wound was visible. Lei continued to run a diagnostic on her patient, burning through potential ailments.

"I'm moving him to the truck. I'll be back to help you stabilize him." She and a nearby officer picked up the patient and lifted him while they waddled toward the ambulance.

"Clean through," the officer said. "I'll be fine. Sergeant Morales—" He hissed as I cut away the fabric from the wound. I didn't think the three villains had guns, which meant this had come from friendly fire. Somebody on his squad had screwed up. It shouldn't make me feel better, but I was glad to see even people with training had off days.

He grabbed my wrists, his eyes wincing as I pressed gauze against the wound. "Morales, he was thrown. He needs help."

The officer pointed down an alley. I should have waited for Lei to return. She'd cuss me out for acting like a rogue cowboy. I pressed the man's hand over the wound. "Keep pressure. When my partner gets back, tell her I went in that direction."

I stood up, stealing a glance at the chaos these goons unleashed. There was no bank, no money, no revenge, just blatant destruction of public property. At least when an evil mastermind waged war on his arch-nemesis, it had a reason. These idiots wanted attention, like a toddler throwing a tantrum.

Keeping my head down, I ducked and weaved through the cars, staying clear of the debris they hurled at the cop cars. At least as I hugged my back against a dump truck, the cops had stopped firing. Somebody must have finally spread the word that a dozen bullets were no better than one. I was glad to see that even Leos could learn.

Covering my head, I made the final dash into the alley. The moment I entered the tight space, the volume of fighting diminished. Looking backward, I couldn't imagine how a man had been thrown this far. My gut tingled, and that usually meant I was about to find a problem I couldn't fix. So far, death was the only thing I couldn't solve. I know, hard to believe.

"Morales," I shouted. "Are you in here?"

The shoeless foot stuck out from a heap of trash bags. If he had been hurled into the pile, perhaps they had broken his fall. I didn't believe it was possible, but I didn't want to find a body. As I skid to my knees, I tore at the bags, finding the officer underneath. Morales couldn't be older than twenty-eight or twenty-nine. He'd never see thirty.

"Dammit."

I pressed fingers against his throat. The familiar thumping was nowhere to be found. I prepared to start rounds of CPR when a series of loud thuds came storming through the alley.

"Cop man, go bye-bye."

Big *and* dumb.

"You go bye-bye."

"Not today, you piece of trash."

Right now, Vanguard didn't need a medic—it needed a hero.

15

I EYED MORALES' BODY AS I GOT TO MY FEET. IT WAS BECAUSE of this towering ogre that this officer wouldn't see his next birthday. The ring on the man's finger meant somewhere a spouse waited anxiously for him to come home from his shift. If he had kids, they'd grow up without their father.

"Little man angry."

I growled, the rage making it impossible to string together a coherent sentence of obscenities.

Dozer stood nine feet tall, and with each thunderous stride, he cleared several yards. I don't know if he came looking for the missing officer or if the brute had been off causing mayhem elsewhere before returning to his companions. As he picked up speed, I didn't have time to ponder the question.

I tried to catch the oversized boot as it kicked into my

gut. I grossly underestimated the man's strength. The world spun, incoherent as I braced for impact. The wall collapsed around me as I bust through a layer of brick and support beams in the building. My back arched as I folded backward around a pipe. If I had been an average man, he'd have crushed me, a flesh sack filled with pulverized bones.

But I wasn't average.

I skipped checking for broken limbs. I'd be bruised, and for the next few days, I might need to take ice baths, but unlike Morales, I'd live. Shaking off the rubble, I flexed my muscles, drawing my fingers so tightly into a fist my entire hand ached.

Flames danced along my knuckles. For a moment, it rippled along my arms, causing my uniform to smolder before it vanished. While I couldn't rely on the flames, Prometheus' suit responded. The black liquid flashed along my forearms, swallowing my uniform until all that remained was the black and gold skintight suit.

With one hand on the pipe, I pulled it free, causing more of the ceiling to collapse. Stepping to the edge of the hole, I watched as Dozer passed by, thinking his death toll had gone up by one. The smug expression on his face made my blood boil. He was satisfied with yet another death.

"Hey," I shouted, "dumb ass."

I jumped from the second story. The goliath turned around, his eyes wide as he caught sight of a costumed vigilante. The sound of his pea brain trying to process the newcomer was almost audible. I might consider it an unfair fight if we were doing the crossword, but as I prepped for a slugfest, I wasn't entirely sure I'd be the victor.

"Squish little man."

"You can try," I mumbled.

He took a step forward, and I spun about with the pipe. The tip caught him along the jaw, his head jerking to the side. Before he could react, I pulled back and jabbed it into his stomach. He let out a roar as he snatched the pipe, tossing it to the side. Well, so much for having a weapon advantage.

Dozer charged.

Squatting low, I brought both hands together and swung up. I landed a blow in his groin. It should have stopped him, or at least caused a yelp. Instead, his knee plowed into my chest, sending me flying once more.

I spun about, landing on my stomach. Digging my fingertips into the pavement, I turned, ready to face him head-on. His expression was almost priceless. He hadn't faced a worthy opponent since the depowering. I was going to whip his ass.

I might revel in the idea of being able to trade blows with Dozer, but anger coated every action. To my right, buried in a heap of trash, a man lay dead. Somewhere a boot missed its owner. His sock, with a hole in the heel —*that* made me angry. Morales wanted to protect the city.

Now, he'd become a memory, another name on a tombstone.

I rose, the fire rolling down my arms. As a medic, I couldn't bring him back from the dead. But as a hero, I could avenge him, carry on his work.

"Morales." His name served as a reminder. Then it transformed into a battle cry. "Morales!"

The fire stopped rolling and poured out of my body. I went from an overly strong brute to a living matchstick. There was no chance to marvel at the sensation, the warmth radiating from the layers of fire hovering an inch from my skin. The heels of my boots lightened until my toes left the pavement. Whether because of the fire or some additional superpower, I levitated off the ground.

"For Morales," I whispered.

Dozer picked up a dumpster and chucked it. It weighed almost nothing as I snatched it out of the air. Spinning from the momentum, I let it go, lobbing it at the deadly idiot. He smacked it out of the air as he ran toward me, fist drawn back, ready to pulverize.

Flying might be cool. It could very well be the most amazing thing to ever happen, but it didn't come with an instruction manual. I leaned to the side and then attempted to will myself out of the way. Neither moved me out of the way of Dozer's fist.

I caught his enormous fist. I dug the balls of my feet into an invisible ground. The suit pushed back, slowing his fist, keeping me from propelling down the alley as I struggled to stay upright. My hand barely wrapped around his pointer finger, dwarfed in comparison.

"No heroes." The idiot couldn't comprehend that there was a good guy with abilities. His mistake.

"Yes, heroes." Snap. His pointer finger broke at the knuckle. He howled, but before he could shake me free, I repeated the maneuver with his pinky.

He swatted at my head with his free hand. I ducked and then launched myself upward. Whatever sentience Prometheus' suit contained, it worked to keep me safe. If it controlled the flying, then I wanted access to the fire.

Punching both fists forward, a fireball slammed into Dozer's chest. The tight t-shirt burned away, leaving scorch marks on his skin. Turning over my hands, fiery orbs pooled in my hand. Finally.

Chucking the smaller orbs, they exploded on impact, causing Dozer to hold up his mangled hand to protect his face. They were a nuisance, but they weren't going to stop the man. He blindly reached out, jumping into the air. His hand closed around my ankle, dragging me out of the air.

"Dead hero."

He swung, slamming me face-first into the brick buildings. What started as a distant pain grew into a throbbing ache. I might have strength and endurance, but this was going to add up. I tucked myself into a ball and forced the fire out of my body. The explosion rocked the alley, sending bags of trash into the air. Dozer's hand retreated as he cradled the blistering flesh.

"Hand ouch."

"More ouch," I spat.

The fire thickened, pouring from my wrists until my hands were barely visible. Thrusting them forward, a stream of fire hammered against Dozer's chest. Washing over his body, he nearly vanished in a sea of heat. I didn't want to kill the brute. It'd be a mercy to end the pain. He needed to beg for death before I relented.

The wall collapsed as he stumbled to the side. I swiped my hands out wide, the fire around my body turning off like a light switch. I dropped the few feet, heels cracking the pavement.

"Dozer hurt," he whimpered. "Ouch. Ouch."

Good. He was nearly naked, bits of fabric scorched into his skin. There were few pains worse than being burned. Having the skin excised was one of them. Even after this was over, there would be a new layer of hell waiting for him.

"I should kill you," I hissed.

I stormed over to the man, climbing on his body. He attempted to bat me away, but he barely lifted his arm. The groan each time I touched his skin gave me far more satisfaction than it should have.

The first punch to his jaw bordered on orgasmic. I slammed my fist into his face a second time. A tooth flew from his mouth, blood dripping down his lip. The third strike was for Morales. The fourth for his family. The fifth was for those who would lower him into his grave.

Dozer's face was a mismatch of dark blue and purple bruises. With a few more strikes, I'd jog his brain hard enough he'd go unconscious. Permanent brain damage might be satisfying, but if he slipped into a coma, it'd be an end to his suffering. It wasn't the best motivation to leave him alive, but it drew a line in the sand.

"I'm a hero," I said, needing to remind myself. Heroes didn't kill. Even if there was a good reason, I had to back away to avoid slipping down the gray slope. There was an allure, a desire to rid the streets of scum. For a moment, I understood the difficulty heroes faced and the decision they needed to make with every confrontation.

"Xander, are you down there?"

Lei stood at the mouth of the alley. Beyond her, a duo of leather-clad vigilantes jumped the overturned cars. Reinforcements had arrived, and for now, that meant my job was done. Even if I willed the suit away, I couldn't explain how an ordinary man bested this behemoth. For now, I'd have to abandon my partner.

The fire roared to life, bursting from my body like a tiny bomb erupted. Reaching into the sky, I soared upward, leaving the alley behind. Flying through the sky like a rocket, access to these newfound abilities had me wondering if it was time to seek Smoke.

"I'm coming for you."

———

Flying into Vanguard City, I always peered out the window of the airplane. The lights below were always an amazing sight. Without the individual people, it appeared as a modern marvel. The city had a peaceful quality from a distance. It had been so long since I had that distance from the activities on the street I forgot the beauty.

For the last eight hours, I did what heroes do. I responded to every disturbance. A mugging thwarted. A bank robbery prevented. A dozen explosives disarmed. With each victory, I got more comfortable with these new abilities. The suit served as my silent bodyguard, stopping villains from doing me any actual harm. Meanwhile, I wielded fire like a human flamethrower.

Part of me wanted to descend into the city, leaving a trail of fire lighting up the sky. Hovering outside Aiden's window, he'd finally be able to ask his questions. Once he got the story, I'd pull off the mask, revealing that the only powered hero in Vanguard City was the same man who wrapped him in his arms as he snored through his alarm.

The fantasy fell away as Hellcat's warning echoed in my ear. It'd be easy to broadcast my identity. But the moment the villains discovered my mundane life, I'd put everybody I held dear in jeopardy. Did Griffin think about these things as he turned the pages of his comics? The burden resting on the shoulders of heroes was growing clearer the longer I played the role.

With a long sigh, the muscles along my shoulders relaxed. The fire drained away, the orange glow diminishing until it was barely visible in the night's sky.

The whoosh of air passing by as I fell was almost deafening. I had a minute of freedom before I needed to worry about the sudden stop at the end of my descent. With my arms spread out, I slowed the fall. I probably shouldn't press my luck, but after a day of wielding the gifts, I needed to know they were under my control.

My arms pulled in tight and I leaned forward, diving toward the city below. It started with the city being nothing more than a distant memory. For a moment, it appeared as if I'd never fall far enough to reach the tops of buildings. The streets below approached, gaining speed with every second I held my positions.

Curling my fingers into fists, the fire roared to life. Now the streets came into view, and with a tail of fire in my wake, I sped my fall. At the last moment, with only a few feet to spare, I turned up, soaring between cars, around stop lights and turning from one street to the next.

It was probably flashier than necessary, but I wanted the people of Vanguard City to see the proverbial light. While the city held its breath, hoping to survive another night, let them see even a shimmer of hope. I might not be able to stop a full-scale invasion or protect the city from the League of Evil if they mobilized, but I'd try.

The momentum carried me up the side of the old building as the flames faded. I cursed myself, realizing I was going to fall short of my graceful dismount. Reaching, my fingers barely curled over the edge of the roof. Suspended above the city below, I prayed that nobody snapped a photograph and uploaded it to the HeroApp™.

"You just had to show off."

It wasn't long ago I hung in the same position, worried I'd fall into a river. Before, I couldn't pull myself to safety. Where my muscles failed me the last time, now I hardly flexed as I dragged myself onto the roof. Spinning around, I planted my butt on the ledge.

A mile above the city, it appeared peaceful. In the grand scheme, Vanguard City made up a tiny blip on the planet. But here, in the thick of it, the city had a vibrancy to it. Even with the threat of villains looming around every corner, its citizens continued as if nothing had changed. Lovers walked hand-in-hand toward the cineplex while the bar across the street boasted a lively crowd, with music flooding the streets every time the door opened.

I promised myself another ten minutes before I called it a night. Eventually, I'd need to go home and crawl into bed. The pounding from Dozer resulted in more than a few bruises, and they ached. I couldn't fathom how heroes did this night after night. Sure, the rich ones didn't need to go to a job, but they couldn't all be wealthy playboy millionaires.

"Ibuprofen isn't going to solve this." Admitting I hurt made the pain worse. I hoped the stamina came with an uncanny healing ability, but I feared I was asking too much.

The brick struck the space between my shoulders. If it had been earlier in the day, I might not have noticed. But it made the pain worse. When I turned on my perch, I blocked the second brick.

"Can I help you?"

Hellcat. A disgruntled vigilante holding a quarterstaff replaced her normal sarcastic self. Storming closer, she let the metal rod drag against the roof, squealing with every step. "You crossed the line."

The accusation had me rewinding the last twenty-four hours, and for the life of me, I couldn't recall anything that'd piss her off. I had to assume somebody named Hellcat must be easy to anger.

"Is this about the fight earlier?"

"You confirmed what they already thought."

She jerked her arm, the staff sliding forward, jabbing me in the shoulder. "We're out there busting our asses. People without abilities are dying trying to protect the city. And you..."

The words ended in a growl.

"What is your problem?"

"How could you kill him? There's no coming back from that."

"Kill who?"

My confusion punched a hole in her anger. Her eyebrow lifted for a moment before her jaw tightened and the curves of her face hardened. "Are you playing dumb?"

"This isn't me playing."

"You didn't fight Dozer?"

I nearly choked on my tongue. "Dozer's dead?" The line in the sand had been drawn, and I thought I stopped short. Was it the last punch? Had that been the one that turned me from well-intentioned to evil-doer?

"I went looking for Sergeant Morales." I tried to recall the specifics as my mind continued rushing to the conclusion that I killed the brute. I had been careful. Or had I? I swore he was breathing when I left. Did it happen after I left?

"Did you kill Dozer?"

"I—" I wanted to protest, to rally against the accusation. But I the doubts stepped in. "I don't know."

"You don't remember snapping his neck?"

Whoa. Wait. I might have crushed his jaw, but there was no way he'd be breathing if that happened. "I knocked the daylights out of the man, but"—this I could say with confidence— "I did *not* snap his neck."

Hellcat pulled the staff away, the end clacking against the roof as she put her weight on the slender piece of metal. Despite my proclamation of innocence, she didn't seem entirely convinced.

"I didn't—"

"I believe you."

"But—"

She held up a hand, silencing me. "Officers saw you trading blows with Dozer. There were witnesses, a lot of them. When the dust settled, he was dead."

"How?" Jesus. I thought having powers might make life easier. I did the right thing, the heroic thing, but nothing about this life turned out simple. Heroes were quickly gaining my respect.

"Not how," she said. "Who. Somebody went down that alley after you left. They snuck in and killed him. It's not a coincidence."

"You think?" I rarely bought into conspiracy theories. Which is odd considering the Illuminati once took over Europe, lizard men replaced members of Congress, and the Egyptians built a pyramid on the moon. Crap, I was in the middle of a conspiracy.

"Has there been anybody you've seriously irked?"

"Have we met? There's a chance it could be my third-grade teacher. I have a long list of people who—"

"Is she strong enough to snap Dozer's neck?"

Oh, yeah. Mrs. Hannaford probably didn't have the upper-body strength for that. My fourth-grade teacher, however. Ms. Simpson flat out told nine-year-old me she'd get her revenge someday. Thankfully the cigarettes—

"Smoke." The name slipped from my lips before I digested the implications.

Hellcat stiffened at the man's name. With a flick of her wrist, the staff shrunk into a short metal bar. Sliding it into a hip holster, she turned around, walking away.

"You're leaving?"

"You're going to lie low. I mean really low."

"That's it?"

"I need to speak with the others. I'll reach out once they confirm it. We're going to need your help to stop him."

She couldn't see it, but I nodded anyway. "Count me in. And thanks."

Hellcat looked over her shoulder. "For what?"

"For believing me."

With a slight nod, she dashed to the edge of the building and leapt to the streets below.

My night had officially gone down the drain.

16

"Is this thing on?"

"You're using the wrong camera."

"Can you hear me?"

"I can hear you."

"I can't hear you."

"Bernard, when did you become my grandparents?"

"*That* I heard."

I buried my face in my palms, slowly dragging them down. From my tablet's vantage point on my coffee table, I made sure Bernard saw the whites of my eyes as they rolled back into my skull. How was this man allowed to run the entire public relations department for the world's premiere superhero team?

"I know you hate texting *and* phones. Do you even own a computer? Bernard, do you still own a pager?"

He held his phone far enough away. I could tell he wasn't wearing a shirt. The man was the definition of barrel-chested and had enough chest hair he must trim it. I caught myself gawking, and my face grew warmer than when my body was covered in alien fire.

"I'd show you the rest, but I don't think your cheeks can get any redder." He laughed. "Nope, I was wrong."

"Why did we date?"

"I'm old, so my memory might be shot. But I don't remember us going on many dates."

Two men, emotionally unavailable when they met. There are nights when I'm alone in bed that I wonder what might have been. Thankfully, the decision to transition from ferocious sex fiends into friends had been mutual. There weren't many men in my life I could say I loved unconditionally, but Bernard had made the cut despite my efforts to push him away.

Years ago, I hadn't been ready for anything more than friends with benefits. Thankfully, things had changed. *I* had changed. The thought of Aiden snoring as he buried his face in my chest made me smile.

"I don't know why I put up with you."

"Yeah," he laughed, "you do."

Deep sigh. "I do."

I nearly came clean and confessed. It'd be so easy to tell Bernard that I was the infernal Blaze. He'd shimmy to the edge of his couch and listen as I unburdened my life. That was the nature of Bernard. I'd screw up. He'd ground me. When I came to my senses, he'd be waiting.

This burden could only be carried by one.

"You're getting that serious face."

"I had a rough day at work." It wasn't a lie. I had become one of the many Americans working two jobs. I'd have to ask Hellcat who signed my paychecks.

"So, I saw the news. Everything okay?"

No, not really. "Yeah."

"Say it again. Maybe you'll convince me."

"Ever try to do the right thing, and it bites you in the ass? You know me, keep my head down and do what I'm good at. I tried sticking my neck out—"

"Uneasy is the head that wears a crown."

"You did not just quote Shakespeare at me."

He launched into a speech about how the bard had a poignant line for every situation. While he relived his college literature class, my phone buzzed.

A: Not going to respond? I'll keep texting.

I made the mistake of telling a would-be reporter I was having a bad day and not giving him the full scoop. Hellcat didn't explain the implications of putting on the mask. She skipped the part where a secret erected a wall that kept everybody at arm's length.

X: Work. I got reprimanded for something I didn't do. Same shit, different day.

"You call me so you can stare at your phone?"

"Sorry, it's Aiden."

"Look, I'm flattered you called me. But..." Bring on the sagely advice of Bernard. "It's not me you want telling you everything will be okay."

"Nobody can replace you."

"I know. Be happy that I'm willing to share you." I smiled. Bernard might be the healthiest relationship I had. But perhaps it was time to change that. Eyeing my phone, I watched as the three dots appeared as Aiden replied.

"Thanks, Poppa Bear."

He swore as he dropped the phone, the video cutting out as it struck the floor. I watched my phone as the dots continued flashing, wondering if Aiden was writing a novel.

A knock sounded from the door next to my couch. It was too late for company. The suit flashed, swallowing my briefs and t-shirt. It'd be hard to explain if it was Ms. Zanella knocking on the wrong door again.

As I moved to the door, I looked at the phone again, watching it like a hawk. I leaned in, putting my eye against the peephole. I feared a villain had followed me home, but it was worse, much worse. Aiden scowled at the door, holding up his phone.

Before I could argue with the semi-sentient costume, it vanished back into my skin. At least it knew the difference between Aiden and a supervillain.

I removed the bolt and opened the door. I eyed my

phone again, trying to make sense of what was happening. Aiden reached into the pocket of his hoodie, pulling out his phone. He held up his finger before punching away at the keys. With a slight blip, he nodded his head in my direction.

My phone beeped.

A: It sounded like you needed a hug.

I nodded.

Aiden pushed his way inside, kicking the door shut. One hand snaked behind my back while the other pulled my head to his shoulder. I might be a few inches taller, but as he tightened his hold, he felt like—home. Those limbs, bulging with muscle, had a power of their own. I let out a long sigh, relaxing my shoulders as I rested hands on his hips.

Kissing the top of my head, he didn't say a word. Bernard would have talked me off a cliff, helping me wrangle in that part that always wanted to lash out at the world. Aiden, on the other hand, didn't offer words to shape my frustration. Holding me, the frustration, the anger in the pit of my stomach, it couldn't compete with the comfort.

Here. Now. I grasped the meaning of peace.

"Will you stay?" The words shook as I spoke, not from fear, but from admitting a desire that had nothing to do with my penis. The silence carried on long enough that I worried I had said something wrong. Pulling back, I studied his face.

Aiden's eyebrow raised dangerously high on his forehead. "Oh, you wanted me to say something." He leaned in and kissed my nose. "Come on, tough guy, it's your turn to be the little spoon."

And just like that, my last bit of resistance melted away.

2:13 a.m.

The moon cast a soft light through the bedroom window, giving just enough light to make out the television on my bureau. I should be fast asleep. But the longer I stayed awake, the longer I got to experience this burly man pressed against my back. Each time he exhaled, a stream of warm air worked down my spine. His leg twitched, snaked in-between mine and I couldn't think of a better way to spend the night.

Aiden's hand worked its way along my stomach, sliding under my arm. His fingers slid along my chest hair before he tightened his grip, squeezing me. I don't know if there was a way for more skin contact, but as he lazily kissed between my shoulder blades, I wanted to find out.

"Do you ever sleep?" The poor guy suffered through my tossing and turning. He deserved a medal.

"Not when there is a handsome man poking me in the back."

"You keep backing up. He's got his own agenda."

I rolled onto my back and, without missing a beat, he threw a leg over me and nestled his head on my shoulder. It had been a long time since this piece fit into my puzzle.

"Next time, I drug you."

I kissed the top of his head.

"I don't want to interrupt this moment..." Well, that was never the start of a pleasant conversation. "But I've had something on my mind. One of those—"

"Just ask."

His pointer finger circled around my stomach, barely touching the skin. If he wanted to ask tough questions, he had done a terrific job of luring me into a sense of security.

"Why me?"

Two words. Two simple syllables that raised my heart rate and sent me reeling for answers. I hadn't given the "why" much thought. He was attractive, sweet, and had just the right amount of sass. Did he want me to list off all the qualities I admired? It sounded more complicated than him fishing for a compliment.

"Huh?" Yup, still smooth as ever.

"That night." He propped himself up onto his elbow, narrowing his eyes to see in the dark. "Why did you knock on my door? I can't be the only man in your phone book, so I'm curious."

I almost chuckled. Not at the question, but that it was a masked vigilante that gave me a swift kick in the pants. If it hadn't been for Hellcat, who knows if I would have mustered up the bravery to take the initiative? So why did I stand at the door, fist hovering, worried what might happen if I knocked?

"Before I knew your name..." I prayed I wouldn't regret this little story time. "...you know, in those five minutes. You were the asshole. Here I was, running into danger, and you told me to turn around. Who was this punk telling me not to save people? It's literally my job."

Aiden continued rubbing my stomach. It was a good sign that I hadn't horribly offended him. Yet. I wasn't used to processing my feelings, especially not with an audience. I hoped he'd bear with me as I sifted through the rubble in my head.

"Nearly dying didn't shock me. Let's be honest, it's part of the job, and the way I run my mouth, it's bound to happen. But then this asshole reaches down and saves me."

"You were paying back a debt?"

I rolled over so I could see his face. I didn't want there to be any misunderstanding. My fingers wrapped around his hand, squeezing it just shy of painful.

"At first, I wanted in your pants." I might as well be honest, even if it was embarrassing. "But that's because I take a while to process things. The more I thought about it, I couldn't stop thinking about this man risking his life to save me. Then he didn't stop. Then he put his life on the line to keep helping people."

"Nice save." If it wasn't for the smirk, I worried I might be dancing on the ledge.

"I'm trained to do that. It's my job. But that's how I view helping people. It's a job. I am literally paid to keep people alive. But here is this asshole—"

"Adorable asshole," he corrected.

"Downright gorgeous asshole," I added, "doing it because it's the right thing."

"So you picked my door because of my passion for charity work?"

Feelings. They weren't my cup of tea. I walked through life numb, and for the most part, it served me well. I might never be mushy, but as Aiden lifted my hand, kissing my knuckles, I wanted to try. "Why? I picked your door because I need somebody who reminds me to be a better person. Surprise twist, you save a man from death and he gets gooey."

"Why do you think I hang out at disaster sites? You were my second damsel of the day."

Xander Bennett was a force. It wasn't my ego speaking. Others had made me abundantly aware of how I was a walking storm. There wasn't a challenge I wouldn't face, but—

"While my brain tried to convince me to walk to the

elevator, my heart—" My chest tightened, the words caught in my mouth. If I shed a tear, I'd have to mock myself.

"Shhh." Saved by the tip of his finger covering my lips. He crawled on top of me, his face hovering inches away. I didn't have words to express myself, so I let my actions speak for me. I kissed him as if it might be the last, or the first, or everything in-between. I let feelings I couldn't describe pass from my tongue to his.

Aiden leaned back, straddling my waist. Whatever I said, it had gone from sweet and innocent to devilish. He rocked his thighs, and I realized how my cock rested along his backside.

The moon revealed the upturned lip and lust in his eyes. "If we're not going to sleep…"

17

Aiden snuck a piece of bacon off the plate while I finished the eggs. I never cooked breakfast for myself and I couldn't recall the last time somebody spent the night. My chef skills were rusty, but any man could make bacon. It was programmed into our DNA, much like our need for sunlight.

"Scrambled eggs, okay?"

"I'm not picky."

Good. They were supposed to be fried, but that had gone horribly wrong. Bacon I could handle, but even something as simple as eggs was a disaster from the onset. As I tried to stop them from sticking to the bottom of the pan, I wanted to know why nobody had come up with a breakfast delivery business.

"I didn't want to ruin last night," he said, as if the statement didn't make the hair on my arms stand on end. "But I have some good news of my own."

I dished the eggs onto two plates before sitting at the table. Aiden took a mouthful of eggs before covering his mouth to speak.

"First, your eggs are awful." I took a bite and agreed as I forced myself to swallow them. How on God's green Earth could I screw up something as simple as scrambled eggs? "Second, I have a story coming out in the magazine. Not just any story, but it'll get billing on the front page."

"You let me yammer on all night when you had this?"

He pulled out his phone, swiping back and forth until he set it down in front of me. "It's the funniest thing. My managing editor called me, and we got to talking. I mentioned the story I wanted to do on Blaze."

"Please give the idiot a better name. Heroes deserve something classy."

"Funny you should say that. I got talking to William, and after bouncing some ideas around, I found my angle for the story. It just so happened he mentioned the three powerhouses duking it out downtown and suggested I see if I could find anything there."

I didn't like where this was going. If he had been downtown, he might have glimpsed me beating Dozer until he fell.

"William thought my entire article about Blaze's origin was a good jumping-off point. But he really pushed me to dig deeper. What do you know, my article is going in the next issue of Revelations."

He included the last bit as if it was a simple fact. But it wasn't a simple article, not by a long shot. This moment meant he had taken a massive stride toward a lifelong dream.

"You say that like it's no big deal."

"I mean..." he tore through another piece of bacon. "I guess it is."

"Isn't your dream being a reporter?"

"Well, yeah."

"Let's do this again." I set my fork down, pushing the plate away. "Aiden, what's this good news you have?"

His face turned red as he swallowed the last of his bacon. There was something adorable about the way he struggled to build himself up. If he wasn't going to do it, I'd have to be his hype man, a role I'd gladly step into. I wanted to see him shine.

"Oh my God." He laughed, trying to dial up the drama. "The most amazing thing happened."

"What's that?" I leaned in, resting my elbows on the table, hands holding my head up as I leaned forward.

"My article is being published!"

He threw his hands in the air. If that wasn't enough, he pushed his chair back. Standing, he started a victory dance. Or, I think he was dancing. Whatever was unfolding in front of me would make any man blush from embarrassment.

"Woohoo!" Okay, watching a big man move was like Christmas morning and I wasn't on the naughty list. At least not yet.

I snaked my hand in his jeans, pulling him close. I pressed my face into his belly, kissing his torso as I squeezed him in a tight hug. Aiden's cuteness continued to impress.

"Now tell me about the article."

"Remember how I suspected Blaze was the only hero to keep his abilities?"

"Can you please give him a better name?"

"Of course not, cause that dude is going to crash and burn. He had us fooled, or at least me."

Wait, what? This suddenly took an unfortunate turn. I eyed his phone, picking it up and read the first line.

"Blaze, a supposed hero who survived the depowering, tried to win our hearts before revealing himself to be a villain in a hero's cape."

I scanned through the rest of the article. It recounted the first day I went out to *protect* the city, before Hellcat set me straight. I wanted to argue that it was filled with inaccuracies and speculation, but Aiden had stumbled onto every error I made on my way to becoming a hero. It was hard to refute the facts, but his story was one-sided. And then, he goes into detail about the death of Dozer, including the coroner's report.

"A villain of villains does not make a hero." The last line drove the knife through my heart.

"If it wasn't for William," —I wanted to punch his managing editor— "I'd have been writing some misguided puff piece. When he gave me the tip-off about Blaze fighting Dozer, that sealed the deal."

I fought to keep my eyebrow from rising at the statement. I would need to talk to Sebastian and find out what kind of disaster William was creating. But I couldn't resist playing devil's advocate.

"But hasn't this guy done some good in the city?"

"I suppose..." Aiden finished his eggs. "But does a few good deeds make him a hero? And what about the powers?"

"I don't want to rain on your parade..." Yes, Xander Bennett came in like a storm. "But it reads kind of like a one-sided slant piece. It sounds like you're missing the other side of the story."

I should have kept my mouth shut. It was bad enough to drop the energy as I reflected on his words. But no, I had to say the one thing that would cut through the news and kick him in the heart. Without saying it, I called his pursuit of the truth into question.

I could see the hurt on his face. "Oh, I... uh... thought you'd be happy."

"I am!" I reached out, covered his hand with mine. "But it sounds like William pushed you into slandering a hero. Shouldn't you have talked to Blaze or find somebody close to him?"

"Cause he's been great about talking to the press."

Is that why the heroes stayed around after defeating the bad guy? I assumed they wanted to see if they could land the front page of the paper. But was there a chance what I believed to be narcissism allowed the press to give a well-rounded portrayal? I couldn't fathom the number of apologies I'd have to give Griffin when this was over.

"I know one of the public relations team for the Centurions. Maybe he can get a hold of Blaze for you."

"The magazine is at the presses. I don't know why you're poking at this. I've been trying to get my break forever. Least you could do is be happy for me."

Aiden didn't deserve to be in the middle of my drama between me and... well, me. I forced a smile onto my face. "What if I take you out tonight? Like a good ol' fashioned date. Movie and dinner?"

The damage had been done. "I can't. The magazine is doing its launch party tonight. I'm getting invited because my article is going on the front cover. Another time?"

At least he suggested another date. That meant I hadn't ruined things beyond repair. I didn't know what else to say. He was absolutely writing a piece meant to discredit Blaze. But Blaze hadn't upheld his end of a social contract with the people. Even with this, my alter ego had to sit through all of them.

"I should head out."

He grabbed his sneakers from the corner and started sliding them on, too stubborn to untie the laces. I jumped to my feet, trying to force the words, "I'm Blaze," from my mouth. With two words, I could put an end to this charade and give him the *actual* story.

"Congratulations." It should have been a celebration, but I could barely muster enthusiasm. Aiden believed I was a menace, and worse yet, a killer. These were relationship issues I hadn't encountered before.

"Thanks." With a quick peck on the lips, he turned and left. I stared at the door, hoping he'd return. It'd be a movie ending where we admitted we couldn't be mad with another one, and after a tearful embrace, I'd admit the truth.

"I'm Blaze," I whispered. But the door never opened.

18

"YOU'RE SERIOUS? YOU'RE KIDDING, RIGHT? NO? PLEASE."

When Hellcat called my personal phone, I expected her to parade me in front of a jury of vigilantes. Reluctant wasn't the right word for my arrival. I came ready to fight, to plead my case and prove to these pompous jerks that I wasn't a killer. What I didn't expect was this badass woman discussing my public image like I was a corporate brand.

"Your fans on the HeroApp™ are defending you. But there are just as many that are convinced you're a villain parading as a hero."

"I have fans?" I criticized heroes for having groupies, but knowing there were people rooting for me—I didn't hate the idea.

"You're the only hero with powers. This city is falling apart and we're losing. The vigilantes can't keep up. We need Supers, and right now..." She gave me the once over. "You're what we've got."

"You really know how to make a guy feel loved."

We remained perched on the Bastille Vanguard City had been built around. Standing in the bell tower, the old structure at the epicenter of a modern city created a beautiful juxtaposition. As the sun set, the steeples of the church cast shadows stretching across the plaza. I had seen every corner of this city, but now seeing it with a new elevation, it reminded me of just how much I loved Vanguard.

"Xander." We had never broken from our superhero personas. "The city needs hope. Until we figure out what robbed the heroes of their abilities, we need to rally."

"I'm your rally point." It wasn't enough that my relationship was crumbling around me because of the mask, but now a group of people who barely trusted me were relying on me to right the wrongs of the city. Even with super strength, the burden pushing down on my shoulders was almost crippling.

She nodded.

"I'm not the hero you need."

"You're the hero we got." Hellcat put a hand on my shoulder. "Until you believe that, I'll have enough faith for us both."

She did the unthinkable.

With her free hand, she pulled at the mask covering her eyes. She painted her eyes with black makeup, but without the molded piece of fabric, I had a clear picture of the woman behind Hellcat. With a simple action, she transformed from a vigilante into a soccer mom.

"Hellen Catani," she said while she offered a hand.

I gave it a shake, never breaking eye contact. Maintaining a secret identity had been the first conversation we had. She insisted that we never break our roles. But with a single gesture, our relationship changed.

"Why?"

"Figure partners shouldn't have secrets."

Partners? Had they promoted me from mentee to a full-fledged superhero? Just like her fist in battle, she knew how to land a verbal strike.

"Hellcat. Hellen Catani?" I laughed. "I just figured it out."

"My husband's pet name," she admitted. "When he gets his powers back, he'll be the one who shows you a real training session."

A vigilante and a superhero, I couldn't imagine what their home life might be like. Did they fight to the death to decide who picked the kids up from practice?

She put the mask on and leaned over the ledge to survey the city. "The Machinist caught wind there was something going down in the plaza."

"Is he hiding nearby?"

She shook her head. "The vigilantes have been told to stand down."

"Why would—"

"Optics. The city needs to see their only superhero fighting on their behalf. Eyes will be watching."

"This is for show?"

She shook her head. "You don't get it. We could easily kill every villain we stop. We could ensure they never escaped again. The city would be safer. But then the people would fear us. We'd be the thing they feared."

The far side of the plaza lit up in a burst of light. Looking over her shoulder, Hellcat gave me a thumbs up. "Be the light the city needs."

"No pressure." I shook my arms, forcing the fire to cascade down my limbs.

"Don't screw up or I'll kick your ass."

"Great pep talk, partner."

I ran past Hellcat, jumping from the bell tower. Yes, I jumped from the tenth story of a historic church. Life had taken a weird turn. It only got weirder as the fire wrapped about my body. The concrete below stopped rushing upward. Instead, I spun about, watching a tail of fire follow my flight path.

It was now or never. The fate of heroes rested on my shoulders. I needed to clear my name and prove that I was more than an angry man abusing his abilities. I put Xander aside. Right now, the city needed Blaze.

"God, I hate that name."

"I warned them. If they didn't release him, I'd destroy the city."

Every villain had a backstory. Some were better than others. The police had captured Neon's boyfriend for drug smuggling. Now his supervillain girlfriend was going to level as much of the city as possible until she got her way. Temper tantrums seemed to be a pandemic in the villain community.

"I can't let you do that." I had practiced some hero dialogue. Griffin would be proud to know I even read a comic book or two. If I was going to play the part, I might as well do a little research.

"Who's going to stop me?"

The plaza in front of the church served as the meeting spot for business luncheons. It was a blend of concrete pavement, small park areas, and outdoor seating. On a sunny day, it was the perfect place to take a break from the hustle and bustle of work and fool yourself into thinking you were visiting nature. At night, there the gazebo, where musicians played and soft street lights luring lovers for a stroll.

Thankfully, it wasn't busy, but I needed to keep Neon busy long enough for the handful of citizens to get away. Already her skin glowed as if she might explode in another burst of light. I held my own against idiot strongmen, but a living bomb? How the hell was I supposed to handle that?

"How did you meet him?"

The people were nearly far enough away we could have a superhero slugfest, and they'd be okay. I flipped off the switch, the flames vanishing from my body. I landed with a thud, holding my hand up, praying she wouldn't annihilate me in an instant.

"Jordan. His name is Jordan. I met him in the foster home." If I had a heart, she'd already be tugging on its strings. We all had a crappy upbringing. It didn't give her an excuse to threaten the lives of innocent people. "He'd protect me from the bullies on the way to school. If he hadn't killed them..."

A killer from childhood? Any sympathy I might have mustered vanished. I held up my hands, gesturing the universal symbol for calm down. Inching forward, I tried to get close enough to tackle her to the ground. If I could stop her without a superpowered battle, the world would see that Blaze was more than flashy abilities.

"If he—if the judge had listened. If the cops believed it was self-defense." It quickly went from a cry against injustice to blaming everybody *but* them for their actions. Her skin vibrated a bright pink before bolts of blue light crackled between her fingertips. As she strolled down memory lane, she lost sight of her path. The young victimized girl vanished, replaced by a sinister broad seeking blood.

"I'll destroy everything if they don't set him free."

No older than twenty-five, she screamed. The nearby streetlights exploded. Every flash of brilliant white light siphoned through the air, striking her body. Nothing about this struck me as a good thing. Her feet lifted off the ground as bolts of blue lightning hammered the pavement.

"Oh shit."

Her skin ruptured, unable to contain the energy she absorbed. I couldn't summon the flames fast enough. My arms hadn't reached my face as the wall of blue slammed into me. It launched me through the air before I could turn on the fire and let it keep me afloat above the plaza.

I inspected my arms and found the suit had been torn away, obliterated along parts of my body. The suit worked to fill in the gaps, stretching slowly. It was the first time I realized it wasn't invulnerable. It could take a beating, but either the energy she wielded or the light itself forced the black ooze back into my body.

"Okay, not invincible. Noted."

I was about to fly in with a classic uppercut to the jaw of the bad guy, but she had other plans. A beam of brilliant blue light slammed against my chest. It took a moment, but staring down, I could see the black recede, exposing more flesh. Did she know how to peel the suit from my body, or was this dumb luck?

"Give him to me," she bellowed.

I shoved a hand in the light's way, blocking it for a moment, and with my other hand, moving it in a circular motion, I drew out the fire. Seconds later, I had created a shield made of flames, and thankfully it provided a reprieve from the psycho.

Neon hammered away at the shield until light poked through. The girl's abilities were impressive, but coupled with her anger, she was a ticking time bomb. The city needed to see Blaze win, to see the only powered hero defending its streets. If she could match my energy output, it was time to get close enough that her abilities wouldn't matter.

Hurling a series of fireballs, her hands flashed a brilliant blue, knocking them to the side. Digging the balls of my feet into the cement, I rushed toward Neon. Leaning forward, I pushed my shoulder forward. Crashing into the villain, she launched backward, tumbling along the ground.

It was time to end this fight and deliver her to the police station for jailing. I followed her as she came to a stop. She was getting to her knees when I wrapped my arms around her in a bear hug. Kicking and flailing, she tried to wiggle free, but thanks to the suit, there was no way she'd escape.

"Let me go," she screamed.

The city was about to be down a vill—

The decorative lamps illuminating the pavilion flared,

and for a moment, I expected them to explode in a flurry of sparks and glass. Beams of brilliant light shot from their bulbs, striking Neon, causing her skin to shine a near blinding white. If I had known her powers, I might have avoided the embarrassing follow-up.

Clenching my eyes did little to block out the supernova. Neon burst out of my grasp, batting my arms away as if they were a minor inconvenience. I was about to ask how light transformed into strength, but then I remembered I was wearing a sentient suit that helped make wardrobe decisions.

"I warned you."

She did. She absolutely did. The punch to the sternum pressed my ribcage in, causing my bones to rattle. For a petite woman, she hit harder than Dozer. It proved that a little package could pack a wallop. As I soared through the air, I had plenty of time to consider how I would do things differently. It wasn't until the descent I remembered that this confrontation was as much about winning the hearts of Vanguard as it was putting away the bad guy. Shit. The vigilantes were counting on me.

I burst into fire just in time to ease the impact. It wasn't graceful, but it prevented a face plant on the pavement. I rolled until I smashed into a small newsstand. The gentleman holding a stack of magazines didn't retreat as he blinked, processing the superpowered man that destroyed his livelihood.

"I'll make sure we get a team here to help rebuild." He nodded after most of that came out as a groan. I clamored to my feet, eyeing the rack of newspapers. I let out a growl when I found Blaze claimed more space above the fold than reasonable.

"You're him."

"Unfortunately," I replied.

"Is what they say true?"

He gestured to a magazine. "The Rise of a Heroic Villain?" I nearly spat. "Am I a good guy?" I would have loved to assure the man, but Neon was walking—no, make that hovering—in my direction. I'm glad to see I got her attention.

The man nodded.

"I'm trying." I didn't want to make promises I couldn't deliver.

He eyed Neon before smiling at me. "Kick her ass."

The clerk held out his fist, completely unfazed by the possibility I might be a villain. Was this the confidence Hellcat had spoken of? Could I win back the hearts of Vanguard?

I bumped his fist. "My pleasure."

It only took two strides and a jump into the air before the flames engulfed my body. Neon attempted another blast of light, but that trick wouldn't work twice. The flames ballooned outward, creating a bubble of red and orange light. Shot after shot struck the shield, absorbed as if they were nothing more than a nightlight.

If I couldn't duke it out with the woman, I'd have to rely on the fire to do the heavy lifting. Sure, I could shoot a few fireballs or bring the might of a firestorm down on the villainess. But this wasn't about stopping Neon. It was about proving I was more than a powerful wrecking ball. Pulverizing her in a pillar of fire would be a spectacle and also reinforce how dangerous I could be.

"Dammit," I muttered. "You're going to owe me, Hellcat."

I dropped the shield and dialed back the fire. I landed on my feet and for a moment, Neon paused her assault, confused. It only lasted a split second before she launched another barrage. The fire rippled down my arms, letting me absorb her lasers with little more than a pinprick to my palms.

"Fight me," she screamed.

"No," I said. "That's not how this is going to end."

Clutching both hands together, she shot a beam of light in my direction. My heels pushed into the cement as I braced, accepting the hit. It hurt. I didn't have many more hits like that before I'd have to inspect for internal damage. But hopefully, I wouldn't have to.

"This is going to help him." Her light dimmed with every tantrum she hurled. I wasn't a shrink. I didn't know how to confront her anger and talk her off a ledge. But I understood it came from a place of pain. I'd have to psychoanalyze myself before bed.

"Don't be the reason Jordan never sees daylight."

The mention of his name caused her to freeze. He might be the reason she was going on a tirade, but it was something more than the kid she met in the foster system.

"You're not alone." I held my breath, waiting for her reaction. I extended my hand in her direction, trying to offer her solace. This wasn't my normal routine, but perhaps—

"Who said anything about being alone?" She screamed the words, raising her fists in the air. One by one, the street lamps exploded. The light traveled toward her like before.

"Screw this," I growled.

The ball of fire ignited over her head. I imagined my hands reaching in, pushing the fire down my arms and into the glowing orb. If rational thought wasn't going to help, then it was time to rely on what I do well. Teach me to reason with a sociopath.

I only had seconds before she turned into an untouchable titan. The air above her head burned, liquid fire growing until it was the size of a large truck. With a thrust downward, it slammed into her with a boom, causing a shock wave of fire to roll along the ground.

Not my most graceful moment. I'm sure there'd be an article in the paper tomorrow about me beating the snot out of a villain. No, they'd probably make her the victim.

Villain beats brokenhearted girl. Yeah, that would be my luck.

My muscles tensed. "Another villain?" I turned to a handful of people hiding behind a bench and bushes slowly standing. The four of them were clapping. One let out a whoop, thrusting his arm in the air. Okay, apparently, I hadn't screwed up too bad.

"I told you Blaze is a hero." The woman punched the man to her right. I'd regret admitting it, but Hellcat was right.

"Stay safe," I shouted. In a burst of flames, I sped past a collapsed Neon, grabbing her by the scruff of her jacket. One victory tonight deserved another.

It was time for Xander to crash a party.

19

"You're handsome and dressed for the occasion. Now just turn on that charm." I nearly scoffed at my affirmation. I might be many things, but I'm not sure I'd ever put charming at the top of the list. But tonight, I'd need that more than the ability to beat a supervillain into the ground.

"You've got this."

Standing outside of the gala, I watched as Vanguard's wealthiest walked down the red carpet toward the massive gilded wooden doors. If it wasn't clear, we were in a ritzier part of the city, the gargoyles lining the fifth story left an impression. Griffin worked for a magazine featuring superheroes, but their operation seemed almost piddly compared to the grandeur on display by Revelations.

"I so don't have this."

Before the two women with coats approaching could intimidate me, I started toward the building. I adjusted the tie, surprised at how lifelike the material felt. If I could get away with never buying another shirt, I'd gladly use the suit to protect the city. Being an outcast had to come with at least one perk.

A gentleman at the door bowed and pulled it open. I avoided eye contact, convinced they'd see the hesitation and ask for my invitation. The opulence of the exterior couldn't have prepared me for the interior. A narrow foyer only served as a buffer to a magnificent open ballroom. The ceiling easily stretched three stories, raised in a dome with pillars holding it afloat.

"I prefer villains," I whispered.

"Xander?" Oh dear God, I couldn't handle being accosted before I barely got in the door. Bursting into flames and fleeing quickly became an option.

I turned to see Sebastian taking a ticket from the coat check. A friendly face. He wasn't an ass-kicking vigilante, but in a pinch, Griffin's handsome, mild-mannered boyfriend would do.

"I didn't think I'd see you here."

"Me either." Did I lie? Or did I confess that I came to make amends with Aiden?

"Aiden, of course. Well—" He linked his arm with mine. He was a burly man, but it was the strength in his arms that struck me as impressive. "You can serve as arm candy until we find him."

"Where's Griffin?"

He laughed. "He didn't tell you? No, of course he didn't. Griffin worked for Revelations for a hot minute."

"That part he mentioned."

"Did he mention the giant F-U email he sent my boss? Damien is a force to reckoned with. Griffin didn't make my job any easier. For now, I'd appreciate it if you didn't bring him up."

"Note made."

"It's unfortunate, too. Would have made afternoon quickies so much easier."

"That selfish bastard," I jested. Why didn't Griffin bring Sebastian around more? This man was amazing. I had to wonder what other secrets he was keeping about Griffin. If I could patch things up with Aiden, perhaps I'd ask if they wanted to go on a double date.

A double date? I hardly recognized myself anymore. I was sounding like a love-struck puppy. The worst part was I didn't hate it. It beat being angry at the universe 24/7.

We walked from the foyer into the ballroom, pausing long enough to take a flute of champagne from a server. There must be nearly two hundred people in the room. I didn't know any of them personally, but I recognized a newscaster, a politician or two, and even the mayor of Vanguard City.

We moved through the room, Sebastian nodding to various people. I knew he was important to the magazine, but with all the smiles and raised glasses in his direction, he must be a much bigger deal than Griffin made him out to be.

"It must be awkward," I said.

"Working for a boss who wants to drive Griffin's magazine into the ground? Yeah, to say the least. He'd have me quit and venture out on my own. But you know, stick with the devil you know. Speaking of..."

I half expected Damien Vex to appear. It appeared that Revelations hired girthy men capable of bench pressing a car. Bald with a strong brow, it appeared as if the people flowed around him, keeping their distance. But the moment he spotted Sebastian, he gave a slight wave, gesturing us forward.

"Into the lion's den we go," Sebastian muttered. As he pulled me along, I'd have to ask Griffin how much they were paying his boyfriend to suffer these people. I'd have to sit down and break out a calculator to come up with a figure that'd have me working alongside people I loathed. Lei might be a pain in the ass, but she was a fun pain in the ass.

As we got closer, the suit constricted. As it shook along my chest, I almost gasped. I pulled my arm away from Sebastian to make sure he couldn't feel its reaction. I'd like to say I knew what it was trying to tell me, but I hadn't exactly worked out the nuances of a sentient suit.

"Xander, this is William Grim, one of the managing editors at Revelations. William, this is Xander."

I held out my hand, fighting the suit's vibrations along my wrist. He eagerly clutched my hand, giving it a firm squeeze. Instead of letting go, he stepped dangerously close, running his hand along my forearm, feeling the texture of the fabric.

"Excuse me," I pulled my hand free.

"I hate to be the bearer of bad news, but your suit,"—he gestured to my entire body— "is a cheap knockoff."

"Jackass," I mumbled.

"What was that?" William asked.

"I called you a jackass. I'll be sure to speak up next time."

His eyes almost turned emerald as they flashed green around the iris. I snarled. I might be out of place, but that didn't give him the ability to disrespect me. Thankfully, instead of brawling, like the socialite he was, he ignored anybody he deemed lesser-than.

"Have you seen Damien?" William might want to ignore somebody beneath him, but he didn't stop giving me the side-eye. If he thought he was throwing shade, he had never met a sexually frustrated Alejandro. He'd need to take lessons to hurl daggers with that level of accuracy.

"I just arrived. I'm sure he's schmoozing with somebody far above my pay grade."

"His influence is almost..." William rubbed his chin to prove he was deep in thought. I wanted to bop him on the nose just hard enough to break the cartilage. His tailored suit lacked any personality, much like the man wearing it. The only things that stood out on him were the piercing green eyes and a rock necklace of the same color. Tacky. "...superhuman."

"I'd wholeheartedly agree," Sebastian added before guzzling the golden liquid from his glass.

"And what do *you* do? Xander, was it?"

"Oh, you know, manual labor. I'm sure you've—" Sebastian shot me a look. Fine, I could behave for the sake of his job. "Excuse my manners. I'm a paramedic with the S.E.M.S."

"Hero chasers." His tone spun a fact into an insult. Nope, not going to take the bait.

"Villains, too." I gave the man a slap on the shoulder. "Equal opportunity when saving lives."

"You must see some uncanny things in the emergency room."

I nodded. I wasn't sure where he was going with this. But I couldn't argue the point. My last trip to the emergency room ended with a supervillain trying to beat me to a pulp.

"I'm sure Damien would love to hear about your escapades saving the tyrants from lording over Vanguard City." There it was, the moment where I went from being a human to being a resource. It was a reminder that Revelations dragged heroes through the mud. I might have once empathized with their mission, but doing it now made me a hypocrite. I hated hypocrites.

"And on that note, I should probably continue scouting for local studs." Sebastian smacked his forehead, shaking his head. It appeared that my charm was operating at peak capacity.

Somewhere, obscured by the crowd, a string quartet played. I couldn't make out the tune, but I'm sure I'd heard it on the radio. Thanks to the men walking about with silver trays with champagne, the bar remained practically empty. I conversed with the bartender before handing him five dollars and taking my beer. I took a long sip, emptying half the contents before coming up for air. Now I was ready to mingle.

"Xander?" Was this going to be an ongoing event? Should I assume that at the most inopportune time, somebody in Damien Vex's sphere would call me by name? I gripped the glass, turning slowly.

Aiden's face gave away his confusion. I'm sure he didn't

have a clue why I might have come tonight. His brow transitioned from sharp angles to a soft roundness. He couldn't decide if he was angry or glad that I had showed.

"I would have been here earlier, but I had a previous engagement." Did I give him a kiss? A hug? It had been so long since I cared about somebody I didn't know the protocol. It was high school all over again.

Aiden wrapped his arms around my torso and squeezed. It wasn't a brief embrace. He lingered, and I savored the smell of his cologne and the way his hands held one another, giving him leverage to squeeze harder.

"I'm still mad at you," he whispered.

"You should be," I replied, kissing his neck. "I was an asshole."

"Keep going." A little humor. He gave me an in where I could come back from this.

"I met your editor."

"William?"

"Sebastian introduced me. He's…" I pulled back as I searched for a word to describe the condescending jerk. "A piece of work."

"The lovable, carefree Xander doesn't like somebody? There's a shocker."

"Ouch. I deserve that. But you have to admit, the guy is a bit of a jerk."

"A jerk who got me a staff position at Revelations."

"About that…" Was I willing to risk another fight? There

was a quick and easy way to sidestep this potential disaster. With a flick of the wrist, the arm of my suit would turn into black liquid latex. With a tense of the muscle, I could summon a ball of fire in my hand.

"I don't want to diminish your accomplishment." I could do this. Check my words, keep my ego out of it. A little restraint, and I could navigate the situation. "But your article about Blaze is misinformation and slander." Jesus, there was something wrong with me.

Aiden's eyes hardened, and the tension seized his muscles until I thought he might throw a punch. "You can't just be happy for me, can you?"

"What happened to the truth?" Revelations had done this to him. *William* had done this to him. I wanted to march over to the editor and jab him in the nose. It wasn't a party until somebody bled.

"You—"

I shook my head. "No, Aiden. I'm proud of you. To be honest, I'm impressed with your determination. You see danger as an opportunity. You're not reckless, but you don't shy away from a challenge. And despite all that drive, there's still this sweet man underneath."

"You can't sugarcoat it, Xander."

"I'm not done." I straightened my back. Holding out my hand, I waited for him to reach out. He eyed it before staring me in the eye. I took his hesitation as permission and gripped his forearm.

"You saved me. I'm inconsequential in that. Hanging from a ledge, this arm reached down to save me." I squeezed his forearm. "You left an impression. I couldn't shake you. But it was in your apartment where you revealed the source of that bravery. The truth, Aiden. I thought it was hokey, but what you just put out into the world..." I shook my head. "That was ambition pushing aside a core value."

Aiden jerked his arm away. There were tears forming in his eyes. I had struck a nerve. Aiden might not see it, but I was reaching into a hole, trying to save him from falling. This was more dangerous than dying. I just hoped I could pull him to safety.

"Why..." He stared at the ceiling, trying to stop the tears from flowing. "Why are you so invested in this story?"

"I... I don't want to see you sell your values." Come on, Xander. That is only part of the reason and you know it. I didn't do feelings well, they were harder than saving a life. At least a dying patient had protocol. Right now, I felt as if I were searching for words I had only seen in a novel. "You got my attention when you came back for me. But—" Do it, Xander. Just do it. "But I fell for that idealistic man. That's when I decided I wanted to chase you for more than a roll in the hay."

Violins played in the background as women in beautiful dresses moved about the room. It wasn't the setting for somebody to be crying. Yet, here we were, me making the man I cared about spring a leak. I couldn't remember the last time I admitted I cared about somebody. Not like this. It made me uncomfortable, but if it left an impression, I'd suck up my discomfort.

"I hear what you're saying." He chewed his bottom lip, and in another context, it'd be sexy. But I could tell my words weren't hitting home. "They're pretty words. But something struck a nerve with you, and I can't figure it out. What are you hiding?"

I could feel the suit against my skin. It was ready to transform, to reveal that I wasn't who I said. With a silent "no," it stopped. Hellcat had warned me against sharing my identity. Was revealing it to Aiden selfish? I tried to rationalize hiding, that I could carry the world on my shoulders. Alone.

Try as I might, I couldn't shake the image of him reaching for me. Aiden had risked life and limb. The least I could do was return the favor.

I turned so that Aiden blocked the view of any potential onlooker. I locked eyes with him before eyeing my hand. He scrunched his brow before following my gaze.

The cuff of my suit jacket liquified. It wrapped around my hand, coating it in the signature black latex. He let out a gasp. But I wasn't done. I turned my hand over and let a flame pool in my palm, tiny, barely visible. With a shake, the suit returned to normal and any evidence of my superhero persona vanished.

"I don't understand," he whispered.

"I couldn't risk putting you in jeopardy."

"You lied." It wasn't the reaction I hoped for, but I deserved it nonetheless. "While I was chasing Bl—you—struggling to keep my job, you just stood by."

I don't know what I expected. Perhaps some sort of relief, a hug, maybe a thrill of dating a superhero, but I got confusion and anger. I understood why Hellcat pushed me to keep my identity under wraps.

"You're a killer."

Shit, bad just went to worse.

The clinking of glasses halted our conversation's descent. A man continued tapping the side of his glass as he took to the stage that held the quartet. The jet black hair, tailored suit, air of superiority, all gave away Damien Vex's identity. Without saying a word, I understood why Griffin hated the man.

I half expected Sebastian to follow, or at least be standing near the man as he assumed a position atop his soapbox. I respected him more when he was nowhere to be found. William, however, gracefully rode Damien's coattails, standing in the front row, basking in his master's radiance. I wanted nothing more than to strike the guy in the throat. He was the one who put the garbage in Aiden's head.

"Vanguard City has become chaotic, to say the least," Damien said, projecting his voice over the crowd. "But I'm glad to see that in our darkest hour, we can gather and hold up a light against this darkness."

The room filled with soft claps. Was I the only one who found it arrogant that this man was catering to Vanguard's elite by saying this party was a way of fighting back the chaos in the streets? It was downright stupid, and I had to choke back a snide remark. Eyeing Aiden, I watched as he hesitated, giving a single clap before stopping.

"Tonight, we celebrate the newest issue of Revelations. In a world where heroes have all but vanished, you might think we'd be nervous. How can we expose these titans when there are no more left?" There were murmurs. Apparently, amongst this crowd, it had been a point of gossip.

"But fear not." He raised his glass in the air. "Thanks to our newest reporter, we have found a way to weather the storm. Aiden Scott has done a fabulous job of revealing the dark underbelly of Vanguard's last..." he stressed the air quotes, "hero."

He gave a bow in our direction and I watched as Aiden's cheeks turned bright red. This blogger-turned-journalist had finally stepped into the big leagues, and not only that, he was being honored. It was a massive step for him, even if

I thought it was in the wrong direction. I clapped out of respect for Aiden.

"Tomorrow the issue..." Damien's words trailed off. He seemed to scour the crowd, his cocky expression wavering. "The issue hits newsstands tomorrow, so let's celebrate tonight." He rushed the last sentence, quick to reach the end. Even as his sycophants applauded, he exited the stage. Something was wrong, but he was the only one to be aware. I searched for William and found his right-hand man had also escaped into the crowd.

Damien made his way toward the exit. I grabbed Aiden's hand. "Aiden, something is wrong. We need to get out of here."

"No." With a sharp jerk, he pulled his hand free.

I was about to argue when I caught sight of the black mist spreading along the floor. I'm sure there were a dozen reasons for it, but at a magazine specializing in superheroes and with Aiden, all signs pointed to a supervillain with a grudge.

"It's Smoke."

"I don't know what game you're playing at."

Several of the other patrons were pointing at the floor. They had a look of glee on their faces, as if it might be special effects to help make the evening more enchanting. It was true what they said about the rich. Not one of them had an ounce of common sense.

The mist collected, rising from the ground until it took

on a human shape. A bolt of black slammed into my chest before I could scream a warning. I shot backward, hitting a wall with enough force it crumbled about me. Whatever was on the other side softened the blow, giving me a chance to gain my bearings.

The coat closet. It wasn't exactly a phone booth, but it'd do. Screams filled the main hall as Vanguard's wealthiest citizens found themselves inside a battleground. I wish I didn't have to save them all, but at least Aiden and Sebastian were worth the effort. Perhaps they weren't all bad. Maybe.

"You picked a fight with the wrong hero." I rose from the bed of furs, hovering in the air as the suit transformed. The fine materials transformed into my skintight suit. Black leather hugged my body until it ended with the mask wrapping around my face. It was time to show Aiden that I wasn't the villain William claimed.

"Smoke," I shouted. "SMOKE!"

I pushed through the wall to find that at least half of the patrons had already fled through the entrance. However, like always, Aiden found himself a bit too close to the danger. Smoke was chasing people, scaring them as if he were a kid in a Halloween costume. This wasn't about robbing them, or even revenge. That jerk simply wanted to terrorize Vanguard.

"Does Vanguard's newest villain want to tango?"

Who wrote their dialogue? Honestly, this was straight

out of a B-rate superhero movie. "No. Its newest hero wants to beat the crap out of its douchiest villain."

"Going to kill me?" He raised into the air, the smoke billowing from where his legs should have been. It was the powered way of puffing out his chest, but nothing about it impressed me. "Just like you murdered Dozer?"

Screw it. I launched forward, flying as fast as I could, arm drawn back, ready to slam my knuckles under his chin. A pillar of smoke slammed into my torso as I tried to reach him, launching me toward the dome.

My feet barely touched the ceiling before I spun around. Smoke had met me as a novice, and now I had a few more tricks to put on display. I'd revel in the moment my fist connected, bruising flesh and cracking bone. I wouldn't win by luck. But with ferocity, I was unmatched, and right now I was in a mood and needed to pound something with my fist.

He attempted the same maneuver. A roll to the side and he missed, and even the massive hand of smoke reaching missed as I put on the brakes. This idiot truly believed he was dealing with a rookie. Even the spears of black he hurled disintegrated as they struck a shield of fire.

"Somebody has been practicing. But you forget who you're dealing with."

The fire gathered in my palms as I mocked this schmuck. Neon had been more of a challenge. He couldn't do more than manifested smoke and... crap. I had been so intent on snapping his neck I forgot about the madness in the emergency room. Smoke might be nothing impressive on his own, but whatever gift he had that let him control innocent victims, that was dangerous.

"Get off me," Aiden shouted. I spun about to see him tossing a woman over the bar. He clubbed a server in the gut, forcing him to double over before driving an elbow into his back. Aiden wasn't a shabby fighter, but with two dozen more people stalking him, he'd never be able to come out on top.

"Back up," I yelled. He jumped backward, falling on his butt as I poured a line of fire between him and Smoke's minions. I could easily burn them to a crisp, but Hellcat's insistence on me riding the narrow path of a superhero echoed in the back of my head. I could do this... I could do—

"Shit."

Smoke had vanished within his own aura of blackness. By the time I found those glowing eyes, they had manifested behind Aiden. There were too many battles on too many fronts. I couldn't stop the madhouse and the villain causing them. I prayed the wall of fire held so I could reach the source.

"I told you I'd find him, medic."

Hellcat's voice screamed in my ear. The exact thing she warned me about was coming true. Smoke didn't want to fight me. He wanted to cause me pain. If he couldn't beat me man to man, he'd go after the one thing I cared about.

So he thought.

With one hand, I grew the wall of fire. With the other, I pointed a single finger, creating a narrow shot of searing flame. It was too far to do anything other than make Smoke dodge, but it gave me time to fly at him like a bat out of hell.

"Duck!"

Aiden curled into a ball as I slammed both fists into Smoke's chest. I drew back a fist, hammering his face, my knuckles cracking against something in the darkness. His hands caught my fist, and I resorted to slamming my forehead against the space between his eyes.

"You..." Another crack as something wet smattered my face. "Won't..." I shook free, wrapping one hand around his neck while I punched with the other. "Win."

Each blow knocked away the darkness, and for a second I could see the outline of a human face. With one more strike, the black revealed skin tones. He was losing, and with a couple more blows, I could end Smoke's reign of terror.

Lifting him off the ground, I slammed his skull against the cement. He thought he could come in here, threaten Aiden, and walk away unscathed. I had won. I had bested him and when I revealed his identity to Aiden, it'd all make sense.

Smoke laughed as the black struggled to cover his skin.

"You," —he spat blood— "think you won?"

His face turned. The darkness consumed his face, and I followed his eye-line. Aiden was staring at us as he pulled himself to his feet. We hadn't started the night on the best footing, but as the horror played out across his face, I found myself the victim of a trap.

"Foolish man."

Smoke hadn't come here to kill me or even harm Aiden. He had found the one thing that would strike the heart. The man I had fallen for had all the evidence he needed. He had slept with a monster.

Smoke had won.

High above Vanguard, I must have looked like a flickering star. Any higher and the atmosphere would become too thin to maintain the waves of fire holding me adrift. Hours ago, when I fled the gala... fled. I couldn't believe, even as I pinned Smoke to the floor, seconds away from crushing the villain, I had lost.

Every time I closed my eyes, all I could see was the look of horror on Aiden's face. It was bad enough that he believed Blaze was a killer, but I had played right into Smoke's plan. That jerk had set me up, laying a carefully executed scheme in Aiden's head. He probably killed Dozer to set me up, and then I played right into his hands.

"He's not wrong," I whispered.

I had been prepared to kill. I could lie to myself and say it was to save Aiden. Hell, I could hide behind the immediacy of the situation, but if I was honest with myself, the truth would escape. Xander Bennett was prepared to become a killer. Everything I hated about superheroes, every complaint I had ever made to Griffin... *I* was the problem.

The roar grew in my belly. As it reached my chest, the flames turned a brilliant yellow. As I screamed, the fire shot out in a wide arc, white-hot. The clouds vaporized as I turned into a living flame. My throat burned as I curled into a ball, trying to will myself out of existence.

I failed.

Once I admitted it, I fell from the sky. The wind whipped past, and as I reached terminal velocity, I wondered if the suit would protect me from an impact at this speed. Super strength didn't seem enough as the ground came into focus. With a splat, I could end the tightness clutching my heart. I could give in and let Smoke win.

Stubbornness summoned the flames. My direction shifted, and I flew forward, weaving between buildings as fast as I had ever managed. Cutting it too close, I knocked several bricks free from a skyscraper. It was reckless, but I didn't care. I had been branded a killer by one of the few people able to cut me where it hurt the most.

Whether because he was occupying my mind like a tenant I couldn't evict, or because I needed resolution, I soared down Aiden's street. By now Aiden would have given his statement to the police, ratted out his maybe-not-anymore boyfriend, and returned to his home.

The thought of him confessing to the authorities the real identity of Blaze continued to burn a hole in my chest. I might not be the killer, but it was nearly impossible to blame him. He had watched every blow as I attempted to slaughter Smoke. A dead body was one thing, but he had watched as I lost my temper and used my abilities to exorcise my demons. It might actually be worse.

I might not repair the damage, but I had to try. Slowing, I hovered a hundred feet above Aiden's building. I could stand at his door again. But the moment I knocked, I started a conversation that could end miserably. At least here, it could go either way.

"Stop being a coward," I growled. I wielded the power of the sun, and yet, the rejection of a man left me feeling weak. I could handle trading blows with a villain. None of them could reach deep enough into my chest to touch where Aiden had access.

The flames diminished until all that remained was a dull glow. I lowered until I hovered just beyond the fire escape. A quick flash of fire would be enough to get his attention if he was inside. It might be creepy to lurk outside a man's window, but I didn't dare set foot on the metal grate of the escape in case I needed a hasty exit.

Aiden opened the curtains. He didn't make any indication that he was going to open the window. The tip of the knife hovered over my heart, ready to plunge to the hilt. I tempted fate and landed on the fire escape.

"Can we talk?"

He opened the window. After a moment, he sat down on the sill. The first hurdle had been jumped. I half expected him to be too scared to open the window, or worse, police would burst through the door and tell me to put my hands in the air. Though it didn't happen, he didn't make any indication he was going to speak.

"I never wanted you to find out like this."

Nothing.

"I don't know what I'm doing. None of this came with a manual. There's no guide on how to be a hero. The one piece of advice they gave me was to never let the people you care about find out."

"How long?"

"What do you—"

"How long have you been like this?"

"The day on the bridge when I saved Prometheus. He transferred his abilities—"

"No." He let out a sigh. The sadness filled his eyes, and I

braced for the thrust. "I've never seen anybody that... brutal."

I could hear Alejandro's voice warning me about my anger issues. It had been a problem for as long as I could remember. I don't know the source, but there wasn't a memory that wasn't tainted with the emotion.

"I've always been like this." It hurt to admit it, especially because it caused Aiden strife. Without powers, I was temperamental, moody, and maybe aggressive. But now that I wielded inhuman abilities, the dial had been turned. None of it left me feeling warm and fuzzy.

A superhero that made the man he cared about... scared. It didn't matter that I had been set-up by Smoke. I wailed on Dozer with reckless abandon even though I didn't kill him. The truth had become inconsequential. I had nearly slaughtered two men because I could.

"Did you kill Dozer?"

I shook my head. "But I might as well have."

Aiden mulled over the words, trying to make sense of the complex emotions raging inside my head. I didn't know how to fix this, how to make it so Aiden saw me as something other than one of the heroes mad with power.

My chest tightened worse than a punch to the sternum. There was one choice left for me. I might not be able to see eye-to-eye with this adorable man, but I could rise above it. I could protect Aiden. The tears evaporated before they could run down my face.

"I haven't done much right since I assumed the mantle. But I can start." Bathed in a warm glow, wearing a mask, I refused to sob. I failed. "This is goodbye, Aiden."

Falling backward, I hit the railing and left the fire escape behind. The flames wrapped around my body and I fought to look ahead as I flew away from Aiden. But with a quick barrel roll, I caught sight of the handsome man sitting in his window.

"Goodbye."

20

"WANT ANOTHER COFFEE?"

"Meh."

Lei slugged my shoulder hard enough I should have whined. She might be ferocious, but it was hardly the blow of a powerhouse. When I didn't respond, she switched from intensity to location. The slap on the back of the head got my attention.

"What the hell?"

"Oh look, he's alive."

They had stationed us downtown for the last few days, and it seemed the world quieted. There were plenty of idiots causing mayhem in the city, but other than a few shortness of breath calls, we sat in the truck desperately trying to pass the time.

"I'm trying to ignore you," I growled.

"This has nothing to do with me. I'm downright adorable. Matter of fact, I'm all that and a bag of chips."

"Slow your roll, ma'am."

"Ma'am?" She pulled back her fist, preparing for another strike. "I don't know what the hell is going on, but I want my partner back."

"Where do you think I am?"

"It's been days of you being a rain cloud filling this ambulance. Now it feels like I'm going to drown. I thought it might be a dude problem. A 'sorry, honey, this has never happened to me' thing. But this is worse than you wielding a broken pecker."

She had a way with words. Ever since the night on the balcony, she had given me space. At first, I thought I was hiding my bad mood. Bernard hadn't brought it up. Alejandro hadn't made a joke about my lackluster attitude. But most of all, Lei hadn't taken the opportunity to rag on me.

"Either fess up, or I grab the Sux."

"How many times have we talked about this? You can't keep threatening to paralyze me."

"Says you."

Her gaze turned steely, eyes narrowing without blinking. If she had powers, this is where the beams of red light would shoot out and burn me up and down. Even without laser vision, I could feel the burning. Dammit, at times, I hated her.

"It's—"

"Aiden? I knew it! What the hell did you do? Did you tell him he was fat in his favorite jeans? Ask him to pretty himself up to go out? Did he make fun of your favorite cat?"

If my eyebrow could go any higher, it'd float off my face. "First, we're going to circle back around to the men you're dating. Second, it's none of that. It's kind of complicated."

"Do you want to talk about it?"

Did Lei just ask me to express myself? "When did we become those friends?"

She laughed. "It felt weird the moment I said it. Can you tell him you were an asshole and beg for forgiveness?"

"What makes you think—"

"I'm going to stop you right there. Why ask stupid questions?"

"I hate you. I really hate you."

The smile spread across her face. "We both know that's not possible. I'm too lovable."

"Damn cat lady."

"Mr. Frumples will cut you." She hissed to stress her point.

She turned back in the seat, resting her hands on the steering wheel. Sharp banter without having an actual conversation—that was our friendship. If she wanted it to be deeper, to truly express our emotions, I think I would—

"Did he find out you're Blaze?"

What? How the hell... I coughed at the allegation. "Blaze? That super—"

"Is this where you lie and try to convince me otherwise? You're a terrible liar, so I hope you bring your A-game, mister. Or we can skip through your weak defense."

I eyed the radio, trying to will the dispatcher to pick up. With any luck, a train had derailed or there was a burning building. Maybe if a sinkhole swallowed Vanguard City, I could get out of having to explain myself. First Hellcat, then Aiden. Do I just scream, "Idiot playing at superhero?"

"I—"

"When did you get your powers? Was it a science experiment? Oh, did you travel to another dimension? Did you vanish and study with Tibetan monks?"

I suppose every superhero needed that trusted confidant to share their secret. I had hoped it would be Aiden, but I had washed that down the drain. It wouldn't be Bernard or the guys at breakfast. I couldn't risk them. But Lei, she knew how to handle herself in a crisis. Maybe the universe was giving me a sign.

"The day at the bridge. The alien in the back."

"Wait? I was right?" She gave herself a pat on the shoulder. "Damn, I'm good. Wait..." she turned in the seat. Eyeing the back of the ambulance, I could see her pulling apart the situation. "You were only a couple feet from me while you got superpowers? This is *not* fair."

"Trust me." I held up my hand, summoning a tiny flame in my palm. "It's not all it's cracked up to be."

"Ability to keep my soup hot, be able to fly over traffic, or hell, even the skintight threads. It all sounds horrible." She pulled back from the daydreaming and met my eyes. "Oh. You meant that thing where half the city thinks you're a criminal and your boyfriend wrote an article about you being a killer? Yeah, rough situation."

"Jesus." I dropped my face in my hands. I needed a new confidant. Could I drop her off at the Fire Station or was that just babies? "Have you been stalking me? How did you even figure it out?"

"Oh, in the emergency room. You really should listen to Hellcat about the identity thing." As my jaw dropped, she rolled her eyes. "Your ass got thrown against the wall and left a hole. What was I supposed to do, not peek?"

"You've known all this time?"

"Oh, yeah."

"I'm shocked you kept your mouth shut."

"I was saving it. Someone needs to cover my Christmas shift.

"You're blackmailing a superhero. You realize you're one lightning strike away from being a supervillain."

"Please," she breathed on her nails, rubbing them against her chest. "I wouldn't explain my world domination plans in a monologue."

"You know, they really do that. It sucks up so much time that I debate bringing coffee."

"What are you going to do next, Xander?" The tone shifted. Lei transitioned from her flamboyant personality to her work voice. We each did it, but hers was a stark contrast to the playful banter.

"We still don't know what happened to the heroes. One moment, they're fine, the next they're—"

"I meant Aiden."

Really? Did we have to talk about it? I'd rather let her climb on and give her a piggyback ride as I flew through the city. I fidgeted in my seat, uncomfortable with her ability to stare without blinking.

"You need to work through your crap and win back that hunk of a man." She wasn't wrong. Unfortunately, I hadn't come up with anything that coated over the whole 'you're an animal' sentiment.

"I'm working on that."

"I'll help you brainstorm. Don't worry about that. What about the hero thing? Are you hanging up your spandex? The city has noticed you're missing."

Lei pointed to a rolled-up newspaper sitting between us. I had seen the article. Within a few days of Blaze vanishing from the streets, city officials were changing their tune. Even the vigilantes couldn't keep up with the larger threats. It served them all right for trying to turn me into public enemy number one.

"Somebody else can protect Vanguard."

She grabbed the paper, and with a flick of the wrist, she smacked me. This was our usual routine: her angry, and me being abused.

"If you haven't noticed, there isn't another candidate able."

"Not my—"

"Don't turn into one of *those* heroes. We've treated plenty of them, the arrogant assholes above it all. You might not like it, but you're the best we've got."

"Great pep talk."

"Besides, somebody has to kick the crap out of Smoke. Did that d-bag threaten your man? I would be out hunting right now. Hell, if you stop him, maybe that'll smooth things over with Aiden?"

Had she been listening to Smoke's threat in the emergency room or was she just that good at guessing? Either way, she wasn't wrong. Smoke had orchestrated the downfall of Aiden and me. We could be curled on the couch watching bad comedies on Netflix, but no, he set me up. It wasn't enough to kill Aiden. He wanted Aiden terrified of me.

The fire spread along my forearms, threatening to burn the sleeve of my uniform. The anger in the pit of my stomach burned, forcing its way upward until I feared I'd spit acid.

"Smoke needs to be put down."

Lei smacked my arm with the paper, trying to beat down the flames. "You're not wrong. But how about you prove you're a hero and not a villain with good intentions? Be the Xander I see back there." She turned to look in the back of the ambulance. "Be the Xander who saved a dying four-armed alien because it was the right thing to do."

Even as she said the words, I imagined Smoke's neck in my hands, begging for his life. I wanted the man to suffer, to inflict the same pain he had on me. It wasn't enough to kill him. I wanted to see him squirm as he realized I had all the power. Why did I have to be the bigger man? I just had to be the better man.

"Sure, I'll try." Even *I* could hear the lie in my voice. Lei didn't hide her annoyance, her lip curling in disgust. This wasn't like my usual issues with the universe. For once, I had a reason to be angry. It took hold and turned into a seething rage as I imagined Aiden's face at the gala.

"And get rid of that stupid ass name."

The girl screamed, but it paled compared to the boy's wailing. My muscles remembered the kid's ability to turn himself into a pubescent banshee. Apparently, robbing people had gotten boring, and he had turned to harassing...

"Cheerleaders? You've got to be kidding me."

The half dozen girls were wearing matching uniforms.

It looked as if they had just left a high school football game as they headed to the local soda shop for milkshakes. Even by superhero standards, this was oddly weird, especially for a grown man to swoop in and save the day.

"Creepy old guy to the rescue." It didn't quite have the ring of Zipper or Cobalt, but Creepy Old Guy was probably available as a domain for my fan club. I would have to put that on the name's maybe list.

Work had turned into a non-stop mad dash to save people after a bomb had gone off at the power plant. Chunks of Vanguard would be without power for days. Not that I kept a tally, but after a string of losses, it was good to know everybody we transported today would live. I was feeling untouchable, and Shrieker was the next to be added to my list of wins.

I cut the flames and dropped fifty feet. As I hit the sidewalk between the boy and his victims, I dropped to one knee. I'm not entirely sure why superheroes struck poses as they prepared to fight. I slowly rose to my feet.

Shrieker's eyes went wide in disbelief. *Oh, that's why they do it. A little slow-motion confidence.* I didn't need Griffin to give me his expertise. I was learning the tricks of the trade.

"You? Again?" The wide eyes faded as they rolled back in his head. Apparently, my amazing dismount and posing with my shoulders as wide as I could muster didn't strike fear into the teen.

"Yeah." I smiled as the flames wrapped around my body. "I've got a few more—"

The fast screech hit like a ton of bricks, forcing me to dig my heels into the cement. With a sudden burst, he diminished the flame, knocking the flare out of my entrance. At least being the focus of his tantrum was giving the cheerleaders a chance to scramble down the street.

Flying didn't require pushing off the cement. It wasn't willing myself off the ground. I wanted to be up, so suddenly, I was where I needed to be. A split second later, I was as high as the three-story building, outrunning Shrieker's sonic death cry.

Bricks exploded as he attempted to send me sailing into the building. I only needed to be on the receiving end once to learn my lesson. As I kicked off the wall, the surrounding windows erupted, sending shards of glass in every direction.

Okay, maybe I was showing off.

"Payback..." Fire erupted around the boy in a circle. He spun about, using his scream to extinguish the flame. "...is a bitch." Just as he finished, I fired a bolt of fire, nailing him in the back. The tiny explosion sent him rolling until he stopped on his stomach.

"Oh, did you just get your butt handed to you?"

"I'm not done, old man—"

Propelled by a burst of speed, I grabbed the kid by the back of the shirt. I spun him about as we levitated inches above the asphalt. The boy sucked in air, preparing to unleash a blood-curdling scream.

"I wouldn't." My finger jabbed at his chest, a flicker of flame jumping to his body. His shirt burned, exposing a bit of skin. "Right between three and four," I said as I jabbed at his skin. "Only skin and ligaments to burn through before I hit your heart."

The kid stopped inhaling. He held his breath as he contemplated if I was a hero or villain. Part of me wanted him to struggle so I could school him. I probably shouldn't take this much pleasure in beating a teenager at a game of 'Who was stronger.' I shouldn't, but I was, and I nearly laughed at how smoothly the victory had gone.

"Let me go," he said as he exhaled.

"I just caught you red-handed chasing a bunch of girls. I'm pretty sure you're going to finish growing your short hairs in prison." Not my best dialogue, but I thought it came off as witty.

He gave a slight shrug, testing my strength. When I didn't let go, he kicked his legs, trying to touch the ground. "Let me go."

"What makes you think—"

"I know how the heroes lost their powers."

I froze, trying to determine if he was lying. Narrowing my eyes, I could feel the fire pouring from the corners. I almost believed I could burn a literal hole through him if I wanted. But he held up his hands, the universal sign for defeat.

"How would you know?" I'm not sure I trusted a villain trying to save his own hide. I did, however, trust a teenager to roll over at the first sign of turbulence.

"Notice not all the villains got their powers? We had to strike a bargain to keep them." I'm sure I could recall Griffin making a statement about how some of the bigger villains hadn't shown their faces since the depowering. Nobody had time to question it with all the criminals running amok.

"Let's say I did. What of it?"

He panicked, eyeing the finger poking through the hole in his shirt. Shrieker believed I'd make good on my promise. This villain, no, this *teenager*, thought I'd kill him. While throwing around super abilities, I was content to beat up the kid, to be the better-powered individual. But him thinking I'd kill him in cold blood, that was a blow that'd no super suit could protect me against.

"Are you—" He focused on my fingertip. "Are you going to kill me?"

I couldn't shake him down and *not* be threatening. I could compare the fine line that heroes walked to a tightrope. Right now, I could barely walk on the ground, and yet I had been promoted to the high-wire act. There was no turning back.

"Depends."

"Smoke."

I growled, causing the kid to flinch. "What does he have to do with this?"

"He gets his powers from a magical amulet." There were hundreds of powered people who harnessed the arcane arts. Vanguard had almost been pulled into a Hell dimension once, because somebody checked out the wrong book from the library. This didn't surprise me in the least.

"What's that have to do with the heroes?"

"He made a pact with the demon in the amulet. He wiped out all the powers. The only people who got to keep them pay him."

"He's a magical mobster selling protection?"

"I guess." Of course, the teen dangling in my hands didn't even know the definition of a mobster.

"What do you give him?"

"Half. Half of everything we steal."

"And if you don't agree, you lose your powers?"

He nodded. "I've heard him speaking to the thing."

"What did he offer to the demon?"

"In return for power, he promised to let the demon free."

I set the kid down. He jerked free and glanced over his shoulder, debating if he could outrun me. Thankfully, he wasn't an idiot and stayed put. Unable to drive, and yet he already turned to a life of crime. Something in the system was broken. This is where heroes were *really* needed.

"Aren't your parents worried about you?"

"Foster parents don't care about no one."

Yup, the system was broken. "How about you stay out of trouble and when this is over—"

"You'll save me? Be my father figure? You'll show me the errors of my way? Like I haven't heard that one before."

"I was thinking more like we'd see if a hero could train you to use your abilities. You can do better than scaring a bunch of cheerleaders."

"Oh."

"Everybody has to start somewhere, kid."

Perfect line to end on. I shot upward high above Vanguard City. I felt like I had finally caught a break. It was pure luck that the source of the city's problem revolved around the one man whose ass I wanted to kick.

It was time to add another victory to my list.

21

"What's your next move, Mr. Superhero?"

While the streets below were a bustle of activity, high above the city provided a space to think. It was wonderful being able to remove myself from the noise of the city. When the other heroes regained their abilities, would this become a congested interstate of people flying about? It was almost comical to think of heroic collisions at this height.

"I can't be the first one to know about Smoke, can I?"

Had nobody thought to ask the villains how they kept their abilities? There must have been a detective or a vigilante who already thought of this? With the ongoing panic of the super community, it wouldn't shock me if they overlooked an obvious avenue.

I thought about finding a rooftop and sitting idly until Hellcat stepped out of the shadows. With this information, she could... What could she do against a villain with Smoke's abilities? There were certain threats that required powers. But without her, how would I find the creep?

Bernard worked with the Centurions and their global network. As the head of public relations, he must have some sort of clout, but was it enough to casually control their satellites and hunt down a single man? I suspected it'd be a tall order, even after I revealed my identity. No, I couldn't jeopardize him or his job.

"Aiden," I whispered. We might not be in a good place, but if he cared about the truth, this would matter. Maybe he could get it out to the public. Once everybody knew the depowering boiled down a single man... The thought died as I imagined him trying to have that conversation with William.

"Such an arrogant jerk." People like him and Damien were probably getting off on the lack of heroes. They were reveling in the fall of the mighty. I might have once agreed with them, but it was time to admit I was wrong. Heroes, at least some of them, were part of the solution.

"First, I beat up Smoke, then I give William a piece of—"

Oh no. It couldn't be that obvious. Shrieker spoke about an amulet Smoke wore that gave him abilities. Could it be the same tawdry necklace that William had at the gala? The two men revolved around Aiden, both using him to get to me.

"Dammit." It *was* that obvious.

Smoke had promised to get back at me, to use Aiden to make me suffer. I had assumed he meant killing him, but the plan had been more diabolical. Instead of kidnapping him, William turned him against the only hero in the city. Only Smoke knew my identity at that point. He had used Aiden as a tool to get to me, and it took a scared teenager to show me what had been right under my nose this entire time.

The suit shifted as I reached for my phone. With a quick punch, I tried Aiden's cell. I might not be able to prove their link, but I had to assume his reporter skills would help him connect the dots. If only he would pick up his— He answered.

"Aiden, don't hang up. I need to talk to you."

He didn't say he was ready to talk to me, but I could hear his breathing. He was mad and I couldn't blame him. I had seen the same fear on Shrieker's face. There were some issues I needed to work on. But that was a discussion for another time.

"I think you're in danger. William is Smoke. Don't ask me how I know. You need to believe me."

The laughter on the other end of the line wasn't Aiden.

I could swear the wind died, leaving nothing but the maniacal laughter a thousand feet above the city. My mind raced, fearful that Smoke had already done something horrible to Aiden.

"If you touch him..." What? Was I going to reach through the phone and attack him? I wasn't Diode or Transceiver, with the ability to teleport through electrical signals. All I could do was make idle threats.

"You had no idea, did you?" The arrogant jerk laughed, believing he had won. As anger coursed through my veins, so did the fire. The flames surrounding my body threatened to consume the phone if I didn't concentrate. Anger hadn't done me any favors. I needed a plan.

"What do you want, William?"

"The difference between you and me..." Oh great, another villain monologue. By the time this ended, I could have already beaten him unconscious. "You play at being a hero. I, on the other hand, haven't been William for a very long time."

"Great, your alter ego is a douche bag. What do you want?"

"You'll find out soon enough," he said without the humor. I had ruined his speech. Good, every victory counted.

"Are you going to tell me how to find you, or are we doing this all over a video call?"

"To the point. I appreciate a man willing to march to his own grave and then climb inside. You can still turn around and hide. It'd be the coward's way out, but nobody would blame you. Hell, most of the city thinks you're more evil than me. If they only knew."

William might work as an editor, but he could poke at open wounds. This was why I avoided therapy. I didn't need to be analyzed and walk out angrier than I started. And he wasn't wrong. One victory over Neon wouldn't change the opinions of an entire city.

"This is the price they pay," I whispered. Hellcat had warned me about sharing my identity and putting those I loved in harm's way. A few mistakes as I learned the ropes and suddenly I had become the enemy. This burden pressing down on my shoulders, threatening to crush me. This was the motivation every hero grappled with. Being a hero came at a price. How many would suffer before the cost was too steep?

Simply by existing, I risked Aiden's life. Neither of us signed up for this life, but at least it had given me a choice. I never wanted to be a superhero. The image of Aiden opening the door for the first time cut through the doubt and left a smile on my face. This wasn't about me.

Who is the hero Aiden needs?"

He deserved the man who stood in the shower, willing to put himself second. The anger faded, washed away by a sensation I never thought I'd experience. I wasn't prepared to give up on Aiden or us. I wasn't willing to admit what the motivation might be, to give it that frightening four-letter word. But it was motivation. Aiden needed a hero.

I'd pat myself on the back for a growth moment when this was over.

"Where are we doing this?"

"Where it all started, Blaze."

I didn't need to ask. This journey with Aiden, with Prometheus, and with Smoke had all started at the bridge. It had remained roped off, cutting off the city from the rest of the world. That's where it all began. Only fitting it would be where it finally came to an end.

"I hope he lives long enough to see you perish."

It was my turn to laugh. "Funny, I was just thinking the same thing."

"Where are you?" asked Lei.

"I don't have time to explain."

"Wait, are you doing superhero stuff? Oh, tell me you're having drinks with Sentinel. That beefcake can save me any day of the week."

Leave it to Lei to steamroll the conversation.

"No. Look up above the city."

I could hear a car door slam. She had been working a double, and I had to assume she was working in an ambulance. I could hear Gretchen's voice, her temporary partner in the background.

"What am I—"

The fire flared, creating a ball of fire that filled the sky. I needed her attention. She gasped loud enough to be dramatic. At that rate, I was going to melt my phone showing off.

"When are you taking me flying?"

"Fire, remember?"

"Not fair."

I didn't have a way to call Hellcat, and I didn't have time to sit on a roof brooding until she showed up. There weren't many people in my life I could rely on, but I knew without a doubt that Lei, despite her joking, stood in my corner.

"I need a favor."

"Superhero asking me—"

"Lei." The one word stopped her from launching into another tirade. Aiden's life was on the line, and I didn't have time to start our typical banter.

"Anything. You're taking this hero thing seriously."

"I'm trying."

I wanted nothing more than to arrive at the bridge and trade blows with Smoke. That was the anger speaking, and with Aiden's life on the line, I needed to be smart. He had made a statement the morning after our first sleepover. It would either solve this standoff, or it'd be putting a lot of people in danger.

"Are you still friendly with the dispatcher?"

"Yvonne? Of course I am. Do you know she just divorced her husband and is dating a stripper from CockWalk?"

Lei. I loved her, but sometimes she made me wonder why we were friends. "Yeah, I need you to get her to do a call."

"Is somebody in trouble?"

"Aiden."

"Oh." For the first time in our friendship, she didn't have a quip to give. "I like him. He's given you some heart."

Heart, it wasn't a word I ever used to describe myself. But the more I thought about it, I agreed. Aiden had pulled down my walls and worked his way where few had tread.

"Me too."

"What do you need?"

"I need you to get a call out over dispatch."

"To who?"

I closed my eyes, debating if this was the right decision. If this was the old Xander, I'd charge in without a plan. It had always been me against the world. But now, with Lei, Aiden, and even Hellcat, I was discovering I couldn't be an army of one.

"Everyone."

There was a pause. "Did you just give me a dramatic

end of scene pause? Damn, you really have been studying up on your superhero one-liners."

"Lei!" I barked.

She relented. "Tell me the plan."

"Okay."

22

THEY HAD YET TO START REPAIRS ON THE BRIDGE. THE towers stood at an angle and many of the wires were snapped. They had deemed it safe enough to fix, but that didn't mean it'd be up and running any time in the next year.

In the middle of the carnage—the gaping hole. That day, I thought I might fall to the river below. Now, with a flex of muscle, I'd summon the fire and skid along the water's surface in a puff of steam. The world had changed. *I* had changed.

I sped along the road, dodging abandoned cars. They had removed the deceased, both human and magical creatures, but otherwise, it remained untouched. I slowed, expecting Smoke to ambush me before I reached the worst of the damage.

"What the hell?" I mumbled as I halted my approach. Smoke stood in the center of a circle with a dozen people surrounding him. I had watched enough B-rate horrors to know magical crap was about to go down. Whatever was unfolding couldn't be good, and now with a coven surrounding him, I had more innocents to worry about.

He knew I was heading to the bridge. Yet he arrogantly stood with his back to me. The man's arrogance was astounding, but he had reason. Without me even knowing it, he had bested me. Unlike before, he wasn't working in the shadows.

"Smoke!"

Nobody moved. Apparently, a man covered in fire shouting wasn't enough to grab their attention. The men and women in the circle spread their hands out, nearly touching fingers as they leaned their heads back. This was the part in the movie where something unsuspecting jumped out of the shadows.

Their bodies dropped to the ground, crumpling like rag dolls. In their place, dark specters maintained the same position. Did he simply kill a dozen people without so much as a snap of his fingers?

"Smoke!"

I landed, dropping the flames. I stormed toward the circle until I could hear the eerie voices of the shadows chanting. Finally, Smoke turned around. Past the billowing wisps of black, I could see Aiden bound and gagged on his knees. Him sitting in the middle of the circle didn't bode well, and if this was a movie plot, he'd be the sacrifice.

"Have you come to watch the finale? It's going to be a good one."

"I know you're behind the depowering."

Smoke laughed, that irksome sound that said he had a secret that nobody else could know. The fire erupted from my arms, the anger pushing it from my body. With a shake of the head, I regained my bearings. Pulverizing him wouldn't be the answer. I had to keep my head on straight or I had already lost.

"Aiden, are you okay?"

Smoke stepped to the side, making sure I could see his captive. Aiden looked down, giving a shimmy in the ropes holding his arms at his side.

"You know, I've been better." I'd take the humor as a good sign. He shifted back and forth, but the ropes held him in place. "I might need a hand," he added.

While he seemed unscathed, the shadowy figures continued their chanting. Were they casting a spell? For all the heroes I had interacted with, I couldn't recall any of them talking about magic. Metal super suits, sure, but if memory served me right, most of the magic users were tightlipped about their practices.

When in doubt of a villain's plan, ask.

"What's the game plan, Smoke?"

He grew several feet, hulking over Aiden. Did he just

rub his hands together and cackle? Wow, Griffin would have a heyday with how many stereotypes this villain fell into.

"You haven't figured it out... Blaze?" He treated my name like an insult. It was a dumb name, but the joke was on him—I already knew it was stupid. "Like you, my powers were given to me. Yours were granted to you by Prometheus, mine—" The smoke pulled away from his chest, revealing the necklace. "Mine by a demon desperate to be free."

"Great, I appreciate the history lesson. What did you do to the heroes?"

"Heroes? Oh no, it's not just heroes. I stole the powers of every person who refused to serve me." Oh great, that meant every person left with powers was part of Smoke's gang of heathens.

"Loyalty or depowered? Nice trick." I couldn't deny it. He had done more damage to Vanguard than the time sentient jellyfish from another dimension attacked.

"I hold all the cards."

"And this little group therapy session?" I gestured to the shadows, who continued to ignore me.

"I'm making good on a promise. Power for his release. And once Beleth is free, he will rule the mortal realm."

"So you're giving up your position? You don't strike me as somebody to take a knee."

He paused. Had this fool not thought about what would

happen to his position if he summoned a demon to destroy the Earth? Wow, I couldn't help but laugh out loud. I wasn't sorry in the least.

"I will be rewarded. First Earth, then every planet..."

"Okay, okay, you've shared enough of your stupid plan."

"Xander," Aiden shouted. "Get him."

Gladly.

The fireballs were for a distraction. Three spheres of flames flew at Smoke. I didn't see if he batted them away or dodged them. I summoned the fire and shoved off from the ground with all my strength.

"You think—"

I might not fly fast enough to create a sonic boom like other heroes, but I was no slouch. He didn't finish the sentence as my fist slammed into his chest. It might not hurt him, but all I needed was to push him away from Aiden. First, I had to get him to safety, then I'd ensure Smoke didn't destroy the world.

"Still playing at being a hero," he hissed.

"Says the B-rate villain."

His body slithered around my fists until he was at my side. With a jerk, he redirected my body. We had almost cleared the hole in the middle of the bridge. It wasn't far for people who could fly, but it meant he wasn't within arm's reach of Aiden.

Thanks to Smoke, I slammed into a jersey barrier, crushing the first one before the second stopped me dead in my tracks. It hurt more than a gunshot to the chest. I could work through the pain... or I could harness it.

My body flared, a burst of fiery light going off like a bomb. The concrete cracked, and the bridge shook. It knocked Smoke away, freeing me from his grip. This wasn't like our first encounter. I wasn't a novice, unsure of the powers coursing through my body.

I was a hero.

Shooting upright in the air, I shook off the impact. The smug jerk gathered the smoke until he grew to the size of Dozer. He thought puffing out his chest could intimidate me. I nearly laughed at the pageantry. If he thought size made the man, I was prepared to slap them on a table and measure.

"Okay, suit," I whispered, "let's do this."

I fell the twenty feet. The moment I hit the ground, a burst of light flashed from the suit. Harmless, unless you wanted to see what you were hitting. Smoke swung, the arm going overhead in a failed attempt.

I kicked, aiming for the beast's groin. The cheap shot would allow me to feel his squishy bits under my heel. I don't know if I managed a ball-crushing blow, but it sent him back a couple of feet.

He raised both fists overhead, as if he was about to drive them downward. I stepped to the side to see a smaller, more human-sized version of smoke step out of the shadowy shell.

Smoke's hand shot out, trying to grab me by the wrist. Long before I was a superhero, I was a barroom brawler. A man like this only got his hands dirty if he knew he could win. As I pushed the arm out to the side, I reached through the smoke, grabbing his shirt. With a smash of my forehead against his face, Smoke staggered.

The villain growled.

His strength wouldn't win. But unlike me, he'd had time to explore his abilities. Tendrils of smoke grabbed me about the waist, dragging me forward, straight into his fist. I tried to land a blow, but each time, a shadowy arm blocked my approach. Eventually they tossed me upright only to meet his fists swinging downward. He clubbed me hard enough it knocked the wind out of my lungs.

"Oomph." I hit the street hard enough that it created a crater.

"It's like you got your powers yesterday. Which begs the question, how do you *have* powers?"

"Dumb luck," I groaned. For a smaller man, he certainly hit as hard as Dozer. If I kept him talking, it'd buy more time. Right now, I needed to distract him as long as possible.

"Prometheus," I confessed, "gave me his powers."

"The alien?" Of course, a supervillain knew all about the people he was trying to kill. "Ah, the suit." He said it as if it explained everything.

"What about it?" Buy. More. Time.

"Magic, of course. His species conjured the sentient suits that give them powers. You're a thoughtless brute. Did you not research your progenitor?"

Prometheus knew what was about to occur. He hadn't been speaking about his own death. The dying hero knew this chaos was about to unfold. Did something about the transference avoid the depowering? I had so many questions, but right now, none of them were important.

"Sentient suits?" Play dumb. Let the arrogant prick take the bait.

Smoke continued to rattle on. He stepped forward, driving his heel into my sternum, but I hardly noticed. It was time to have a long-overdue conversation.

Hey, suit, we need to talk.

Would it respond? Was it a living object with its own ability to form words? Could it speak English? This was almost—

The suit rippled. It wasn't a word, but a sensation warming my body. I had felt a similar sensation when I first shook William's hand. The suit *was* alive.

I don't know what I'm doing here. This guy is about to destroy the world. We're the last line of defense. I swallowed my pride and finally admitted the scariest thing. *I need your help.*

Smoke ground in his heel as he let loose maniacal laughter. If the suit didn't respond, I was prepared to summon the fire, all of it. If I went supernova, perhaps I could break through his shields and kill—

A hand grabbed Smoke's ankle. I raised my hands, glancing at between them and the additional appendage. Another arm emerged from the suit, pushing off the ground. Like Prometheus, the suit transformed me into a Tetrabrachius. Whoa, how did I even know that word?

The extra arm pushed off the ground, while the other yanked at his leg. It was Smoke's turn to slam into a jersey barrier. I hope it hurt, a lot.

The fire returned without me summoning. I might not understand the suit, at least not yet, but I officially had a partner. It was amusing that watching Smoke fight, fists in conjunction with his powers was my teachable moment. Now it was time to school the villain.

The fire siphoned from my body, pooling in at my chest before shooting forward. It slammed into Smoke, forcing him to hold up his hands. Try as he might, the shield of darkness was pulverized and he couldn't summon his abilities quick enough to stop me.

"You're done, William."

A tendril of smoke shot forward. The pointy tip would have skewered my skull if the suit's hands hadn't caught it.

It was my turn to laugh. Yes, laugh and make it as condescending as possible.

"You pitiful fool." Damn, I see why he enjoyed it. But I didn't need to stand superior to the villain. I just needed to snatch the necklace off his body and destroy it. A superpowered Smoke would break free from jail in no time. I wanted a weak and helpless William behind bars.

A plume of smoke clouded the area around William. As I let loose another burst of fire, he was already flying over the hole in the bridge, returning to his coven of shadow creatures.

"Dammit," I followed. He was faster, reaching the circle before me.

"Your boyfriend isn't essential. He was to serve as icing for Beleth, a blood sacrifice for the hungry."

He lifted Aiden by the neck, holding him out as a human shield. I could have attempted for a precision shot of fire into Smoke's skull, but I couldn't risk Aiden. I'd never forgive myself if I hurt him.

"You have a decision, hero. Save Aiden or stop the end of the world." He moved until he stood at the end of the gaping hole in the bridge. It was ironic. He stood in almost the same spot where Aiden had first saved me. The hand reaching over the ledge rested on the back of my head.

"Save your man, or stop me. You can't do both."

He dangled Aiden over the edge of the hole. He struggled, but the ropes held fast. Letting his face go limp, he stared at me. His eyes went from narrow to wide. Even from here, I could see the sadness filling them.

"Which will it be, hero?"

"If you hurt him—"

"You'll what? Stop me? That hasn't worked for you yet."

Aiden tilted his head back, trying to throw a look at Smoke. He wasn't giving up. He was granting me permission. Aiden was willing to sacrifice himself so that I could save the world. My heart nearly burst as I realized the man was giving me the okay to let him die.

"Time to choose, Blaze."

Smoke thrust Aiden downward through the hole.

23

THERE WAS ONLY A SPLIT SECOND TO DECIDE. DID I RESCUE Aiden or did I stop Smoke from summoning a demon to destroy mankind? I didn't want to live in a world without Aiden.

There was no decision. The suit agreed.

I flew downward, speeding toward the icy river hundreds of feet below. Aiden didn't scream. He did nothing other than close his eyes. As he plummeted toward his death, I hope the flashes of his life included me. I wanted to be one of the fond memories that made him smile.

"Aiden," I shouted as I reached him. Waving a quick hand over the ropes, they burned away. I cradled him, matching his speed as to not break his back. We slowed until we hovered several stories above the water.

He opened one eye, not convinced I had rescued him. I pushed the flames from my arms and torso, concentrating them along my legs to prevent him from being startled. He turned his head, looking at the water below.

"I don't want to cut this short..." I really didn't. Part of me wanted to whisk him away to some tropical island and live happily ever after.

"Right now, you're one of the most powerful men on the planet and you're asking me for permission?"

I looked up, studying the damage done to the bridge. Being a hypocrite could be a topic of discussion. I promised him to seek help, and here I was imagining my fist knocking the teeth from William's mouth.

"Yeah. I guess I am."

"Face it, we're not always going to agree."

"This isn't debating which direction the toilet paper should go."

"Front, we all know that." He patted the side of my face. Leaning his head against my shoulder, I think being the damsel had already grown on him. "We're going to fight. You have the heart of a lion. Follow it and do what's right. I'll understand."

"I want to beat that—" That was the old Xander speaking. What did this improved version of me want? Aiden requested I follow my heart. I turned from the bridge to see his gentle features.

"I want to be a hero." I choked up at the confession. "The one you deserve."

"The hero I deserve would show the asshole that nearly killed me who was boss."

Could he handle seeing the ferocity? If I had to see the look of horror on his face again, I'm not sure I'd survive.

"Do what's necessary." Permission granted.

"Hold on." I rocketed upward. Flying toward the hole in the bridge, I clutched Aiden. He held his eyes closed, not appreciating the gift of flight. We had our moment, the promise of another chance to make things right. It only required me stopping a demon from destroying the planet. Typical relationship issues.

"Smoke!" I screamed his name as we passed through the hole. I wanted the man's attention, wanted him seeing that Aiden and I had emerged victorious.

"Heroes, you're all stupid. You could have saved the world, but you decided on a few minutes with *him*?"

"Worth every second."

"Fool. Why don't you hand him to me? I'll make sure Beleth puts him to good use."

It was my turn to laugh. It bordered on cackling until Aiden finally covered my mouth with his hand. I took a hint and stopped. Flying overhead, Smoke watched, fixated.

"I thought I might leave him with them." I gestured down the bridge with my chin.

The heroes of Vanguard had assembled.

Smoke turned to Hellcat, holding her staff in hand. Alone, she might not have been impressive. But it was the hundred costumed vigilantes lining the bridge behind her that caused my heart to surge.

Aiden gasped, "Is that—"

"The depowered." Lei had put out the call for anybody capable of fighting to converge at the bridge. I had expected the tech-savvy vigilantes or those with gadgets and fancy martial art skills. What I didn't expect, even without their powers, the heroes had come at the call.

"Why are they—"

"Somebody reminded me, heroes can't do this alone."

I flew over Smoke, landing at the front lines. Hellcat gave me a nod. "Your partner said you needed some help, and I quote," —she made air quotes— "'He needs help to save a sexy beast of a man.'"

I rolled my eyes while Aiden snickered. I don't know what she said that convinced them, but Lei had a way about her. Behind a trio of the Machinist's metal suits, I spotted the Centurions, Vanguard's resident elite.

Hellcat leaned in, whispering. "They came for you, Xander."

"Wait? She knows?" Aiden asked.

"Sorry, kid. It's a superhero thing. I told him not to tell you, so..." She gestured toward Smoke. "You wouldn't get kidnapped."

"Epic fail."

I ignored their banter. "They came for me?"

"We protect our own," she said.

One of Machinist's suits landed next to Aiden. Its hands reached out, hooking Aiden from under the armpits. He shook his head. "No, I'm staying here."

I leaned in to kiss him when I realized there were at least a hundred pairs of eyes watching. Screw it. I pressed against him, wrapping a hand behind his head, pressing my lips against his. He resisted for a moment before relaxing and returning it with vigor.

"At least you'll be alive to be mad." With a smack on the arm, the suit launched into the air, taking Aiden with him.

"He's going to be so pissed," Hellcat said.

Ignoring her, I turned around to see Smoke hovering in the middle of his circle. The specters around the outside lifted into the air, seeping into the darkness around the villain.

"You should have stopped me," he shouted. "It's done."

"This can't be good," Hellcat added.

"It's just one guy..."

The circle glowed, arms reaching up from inside. A second later, hundreds of shadows shot up into the air. I could have stopped him from completing the spell, but it'd have cost Aiden his life. I had made the right decision. My heart knew it.

"You're too late, Blaze," he cackled, raising his arms in the air as he basked in his sorcery. "He's here."

"We've got your back," Hellcat said, glancing over her shoulder at the agitated group of heroes.

The flames poured out of my body with a growl. The flesh of my hands disappeared under the fire. I inspected the other three hands. It took a second to realize that there was no flesh left. I was a living torch.

"The name's Lionheart."

24

Madness ensued. The circle grew, allowing more demons to escape their Hell dimension. Smoke remained perched in the center, basking in the chaos. But try as he might, the legion of evil wasn't making much headway.

Two demons swept Cobalt into the air. With palms pointed outward, I launched a stream of fire, vaporizing the gargoyle-like creatures. As he plummeted toward the bridge, a man wearing a jetpack caught him. They might not all belong to the same team, but the heroes of Vanguard stood united against the threat.

Hellcat waved her arms, trying to get my attention. With a quick spin, she batted a nearby demon with her staff. Another thrust and the end electrified, shocking the creature into submission. I dropped onto it, turning it to embers.

"We can't keep this up."

"The good guys are holding their own," I argued.

"We're human—" The Machinist's suits flew over. "Mostly human. We'll fight until we can't, but people are going to tire."

I had tried to approach Smoke half a dozen times. No matter how much fire I threw, his demons protected him. He was the key to winning this battle. If only I could get to him.

"I can't reach him."

"Not alone." With a spin of her wrists, the staff separated into two batons. As she let the tips touch, sparks flew out in all directions. "We need backup."

"You've got it." The gruff voice stepped around an overturned taxi. I knew the Centurions had joined the fight, but to see Sentinel up close, I couldn't help but stare. It didn't hurt that the burly bearded man had 'daddy bear' written all over him.

"Centurions," he yelled.

Sentinel nodded to the four teammates gathering about him. "This man needs to reach,"—he pointed a metal gauntlet at Smoke— "that man."

Sentinel charged forward without another word. Crimson, Iris, Lightyear, and Elixir followed suit without a word. Forming a human V, they drew the attention of a horde of demons.

I was about to yell a warning when Sentinel ducked

under an outstretched talon. Crimson hurled a knife, striking the creature in the forehead. He rolled, grabbing his weapon and springing back to his feet. It was almost as if he didn't need to absorb solar radiation to be heroic.

None of them did.

Sentinel slammed his fist into a demon's face. Lightning exploded from the impact, much like Hellcat's staff. Had she been receiving equipment from the Centurions? Were they the secret network she always referred to? I had so many questions to ask once this fight ended.

The Centurions had almost cleared a path to the glowing circle, and I pushed off, flying through the gap. Dodging a giant demon, I hurled a fireball toward Sentinel. As if he predicted the move, he jumped out of the way, letting the projectile burn through a demon's chest.

I was going to make it. I just had to clear two towering ugly creatures, and I'd be at Smoke. I tucked into a ball, rolling along the ground before kicking off, drilling my knuckles into the chin of one beast.

The other snatched me out of the air, its fingers closing around my chest. Its jaw opened, bearing rows of jagged, misshappen teeth. The flare from my body dissolved its hand. Fire from my chest bombarded the creature until nothing remained.

Smoke.

"They're all going to die," he said. The words were unnervingly calm, as if he had discovered his inner peace amidst the chaos. Smoke had gone from the type of villain who sought power and fame to the kind who wanted to watch the world bathed in blood.

"Not if I can help it."

The blackness receded down his body until William's naked torso sat exposed. It was the opening I needed. Both palms out, I sent forth a flood of fire. But the perfect white of William's skin broke away as a hand shot forward, catching the fire and extinguishing it.

"Mortals," William's body vanished as claws pulled their way free of his body. The beast half emerged, half consumed him until all that remained was a large beast with inverted legs, lizard-like skin, and a head shaped like a bull. The smell of sulfur filled the air, confirming that this was Beleth. William's plan had worked, but I doubt he understood the price of bringing the denizen to the mortal realm.

"A demon. Sure, no problem."

With a glance over my shoulder, I watched as Sentinel punched at a trio of demons threatening to drag him away. Iris pulled herself along the ground while Hellcat tried to protect the hero. I couldn't have made it this far without them, but they were about to lay down their lives. Too many heroes had died in my ambulance. I wouldn't be the cause for their deaths.

"Beleth," I shouted. "If you want this realm, you'll need to best me." It sounded as if I was confident. But the snorting chuckle with steam puffing from its nose said he wasn't convinced.

"You will be the sacrifice that keeps me here."

Wait, did a demon from Hell just threaten to kill me? I shook my head as I rose into the air. Forget the beast's attempts at witty dialogue; he had already given away the solution to this problem. Nobody dies. Simple enough, right? Maybe if it weren't for the demons trying to kill depowered heroes.

Four fists forward, the fire tore its way from my chest, down the limbs, into focused beams. Its talons reached out, absorbing the fire as if it were nothing more than a nuisance. The suit's arms shifted and, with one more attempt, a beam struck the demon's shoulder. Charred flesh vaporized, flying into the air.

The beast roared.

"Good." All four fists tightened into fists. "You can be hurt."

I flew at Beleth, arms drawn back, ready to smash knuckles into the demon. Annoying editor or hellspawn, they weren't so different. But now, there was no reason to hold back.

Beleth moved faster than his size should allow. I couldn't slow my approach before he snatched me around the neck. Pulled at his hand and, with the help of the suit's appendages, I jerked free. If I was going to be close enough to smell the decay, I might as well brawl like it was the end of the world.

All four fists flared a searing white. He caught my right hook, but couldn't prevent the suit from jabbing its snout. Beleth pulled at my hand, opening its mouth to claim his meal. With a burst of fire, his hand loosened enough for me to slip down.

As my heels hit the pavement, I ducked its attempt to grab my head. With a punch to the groin, I prayed demons had testicles. Unfortunately, it did little more than aggravate the beast. With a kick to the chest, I watched as the sky passed overhead. I slammed into a barrier, pulverizing it as I slid.

Beleth landed on me before I could form a string of coherent swears. I tried to fly away, but the demon caught me by the ankle, slamming me against the pavement as if we were living out a children's cartoon. Each mouthful of asphalt left my bones more and more achy. The suit protected its wearer, but even it had a limit.

I glimpsed a hero being hurled over the side of the bridge. If they were lucky, they'd die. At worse, they'd survive the fall and have their skeleton turned to powder on impact. The heroes were dying. I led them here. I'd carry every death on my shoulders.

William did this.

The anger pooled, gathering in the pit of my stomach in a tsunami of rage. That arrogant prick rendered the heroes,

Vanguard's last line of defense against evil-doers, unable to protect themselves. For what? Power? Fame? An extra inch on his penis? Whatever the reason, his name would serve as a curse for generations.

My fingers dug into the pavement, preventing Beleth from tossing me around like a rag doll. Kicking, I freed myself enough to roll over. I directed the rage, the pent-up anger that lingered behind a thin calm. Willing it from my body, it was less fire and more a blazing light. The ground tore away, leaving a hole down to the rebar. While a nearby car flipped in the air, Beleth's toes dug in, holding him steady.

"Xander..."

Black tendrils wrapped about William's arms, holding him in place within the demon's chest. While Beleth hadn't moved, I shattered the shell hiding his tribute. The source of this carnage sank into the beast's chest, vanishing once again, but not before I glimpsed the necklace dangling about his neck.

The suit's arms reached for the pendant, hoping that pulling it from William's neck might end the battle. Beleth caught both hands and with a foot braced against my chest, he tore the limbs free. They weren't *my* limbs, but the suit vibrated as if it screamed in reply.

"Mortal dies," Beleth said as he roared. Holding my severed limbs in the air, the demons on the bridge cheered, a cacophony of hissing and grunts.

It leaned in, foot and nails digging into my chest. Even with my strength, the weight of the creature held me captive in the hole my powers created. With a puff of smoke from its pig-like nose, it roared again, close enough I could smell the death.

"My legions will roam free from Hell."

I wanted to scream, but I couldn't draw enough air. My ribs were bruised and my sternum threatened to break. I struggled, trying to pull my arms free. Even the fire raging through my veins did nothing to force Beleth from crushing me.

I imagined a respectable death. Instead, I was about to be eaten by a minotaur with bad breath.

25

"AIDEN." IT WAS THE ONLY TWO SYLLABLES I COULD MUSTER.

Beleth's jaw expanded, unhinging until he transformed into nightmare fuel. The fire rippling along my arms did nothing to slow him. I needed one of those flaring moments, but as his nails threatened to penetrate the suit, I couldn't focus.

The darkness enveloped my head. I refused to close my eyes. If I was going to die, I'd see it to the end. Even in death, I'd be a stubborn jerk. The demon's tongue slithered along my neck, a dry crusty sensation that would haunt me for the next ten seconds of my life. It sounded as if the beast was inhaling, sucking in air as if gasping for breath, but I couldn't feel the air moving, just the sensual touch of its tongue.

The ear-piercing scream wasn't mine. The world spun

about. Light, I could see the sky again. The pressure along my chest vanished. Beleth wasn't holding me as I spun through the air. My senses returned, and I had a moment to taste the salty air.

"Shrieker?"

The teenager leaned into the force of his powers. The air rippled, his abilities sending heroes and demons along to their knees. With his back against a car, he braced for the immensity of his own powers. Beleth slammed into a truck, pushed into its frame. Its growls were almost inaudible by comparison. Shrieker had pinned the beast.

Having turned traitor, the teenager was the last person I expected to join in the fight. Had he taken me up on my offer? I imagined heroes spent their days saving those without powers, protecting them from evil outside their control. It had never dawned on me I might actually sway the destiny of somebody on the other team.

Shrieker fell to his knees. The kid had to inhale eventually, and after that demonstration, I didn't know if he had a whisper left in him. Beleth's roared loud enough to break through my fuzzy hearing. He tore away from the truck, reaching back, digging his claws into the car and hurling it at the kid.

"No." It wasn't begging. It was a simple fact. Beleth would not end the kid. The flames wrapped about my body before pouring out of my palms. The truck changed directions, hurled through the hole.

Beleth charged at the kid, determined to make him pay. I wasn't about to let the kid be a sacrifice because of me. It was time to end this battle and save Vanguard City.

I landed between the demon and Shrieker. Holding up my hands, I could see through my limbs. I was no longer surrounded by the inferno. I had *become* the inferno.

A wall of fire sprung up from the ground. Beleth struck it, his nails piercing the barrier, tearing it open as if it were paper. With each step toward the beast, he grew smaller. No, it wasn't the demon shrinking—I was growing. Even the suit wrapped around my fiery form tightened.

Beleth was a symptom of the cause. But it was the man housed inside his body that had created this problem. I could trade blows all day with this demon, but eventually he'd overpower me, and I'd serve as a meal. There weren't enough Shrieker's in Vanguard to protect it.

The wall of fire reshaped, turning into a pair of fists. Instead of restraining the beast, I imagined it tearing through Beleth's chest. I shoved my own hands forward, controlling the phantom limbs remotely. I wanted at the villain inside. Milky flesh rose to the surface and I could see a shoulder, then the neck. With a growl, I tore open Beleth's chest, revealing a trapped William.

Beleth struggled, threatening to break free from my grasp. I couldn't hold him and free William. Aiden's words echoed in the back of my head. I had stepped up to the plate and become the hero. But that adorable journalist had been right. We couldn't do this alone. The admission was difficult, but I was a single man.

I couldn't do this alone.

"The necklace, Shrieker," I growled. "It's time to be a hero."

I couldn't hear a response, not a confirmation or the sucking in of oxygen. I heard the high pitch squeal. A single, short, punctuated yelp from the kid. He had exhausted his talents saving me.

The green amulet shattered.

Beleth howled. He no longer tore at the shield. The circle of magic pulled at the demons covering the bridge. One by one, it sucked them into the portal, returned to whatever hell they had been summoned. Beleth fell to the pavement, determined to claw his way to freedom.

It was mere seconds before only Beleth remained. I grunted, suddenly aware of the pain coursing through my body. I should have slumped to the ground and called it a day. Being a hero meant doing the *right* thing, not the easy thing.

I jumped into the air, landing on Beleth's back. Kneeling, I reached back before driving my fist into the creature's shoulder. The demon had turned into an almost dense liquid, bits pulling free from his body and sucked into the portal. Fishing around inside the beast, I found what I was looking for. With a yank, I jerked William's limp form free.

Rolling off Beleth, I tossed William to the side. I had to

save him, not be gentle with the creep. With a wave, I watched as Beleth lost the battle with the circle, pulled into the depths of Hell. The portal vanished, and it left me unconvinced that the fight was over, that we had won.

Then the cheering started.

Bruised eardrums made it almost impossible to hear. I rolled over to see Hellcat standing in front of me, a hand held out. The fire vanished as I clutched her forearm. I ignored the circle and instead focused on the heroes of Vanguard. Men and women were thrusting their fists in the air.

She shouted at me. "You did this!"

But the victory was short-lived as they returned to those unable to stand. As if the curse had been lifted, those that could fly rose into the air. Holding their fallen comrades, they flew toward Vanguard. A blur of red flew down the street as Zipper helped usher the wounded to hospitals.

The heroes of Vanguard City had returned.

My chest swelled, filled with pride. I might have led the charge, but this wasn't a victory of one. As Shrieker hobbled to my side, I patted the kid on the shoulder. They would remember this moment as the moment Vanguard's heroes proved it wasn't powers that made a hero.

"So, my training," Shrieker shouted. The kid stuck a finger in his ear, wiggling it about. He held his nose and puffed his cheeks as he tried to speed up recovering his hearing. "When do we start?"

I held his shoulder as I watched the best of mankind do what they do best. For the first time, I finally understood what it meant to be a hero. I could already hear Griffin's voice in my ear as I ate humble pie and changed my opinion about superheroes.

"We already have, kid." With a step forward, I stumbled. Hellcat held me upright, putting my arm over her shoulder. With a nod, I smiled at my designated mentor. "We already have…"

EPILOGUE 1

"...AND THE INCIDENT IN THE SUBWAY?"

I let out a growl as I squeezed the cushion in my lap. Three months of saving people, three months of mastering my abilities, despite that, a B-rate villain had got the drop on me. When Dune got away, turning to sand and fleeing through an access panel, I had lost my temper.

"He's not even a *good* villain. I can't believe I let him get away."

The man sitting opposite of me, across a dark-colored coffee table, pulled the glasses from his face. He rubbed the bridge of his nose, a sign that I was about to receive a lecture I had already heard. Sliding his glasses into his pocket, he relaxed, taking a deep breath while he studied me.

"Xander." Therapist to the heroes. The man knew all of

our identities. One person housed enough information to shake the entire superhero community. Thankfully, he might be the only secret more closely guarded than our own identities.

"What am I about to say?" He rested his hands in his lap, leaning back in the leather chair. Ugh, he was about to do it again. Doctor Solaris wanted me to do the work myself. I think he might be the only person more aggravating than Shrieker. Tim was by far the most talkative man on the planet, and training him required the patience of a saint.

"I can't expect to win every battle. That I need to stop putting the pressure on myself to be perfect. Some victories aren't instant."

"So you *do* listen to me."

"Once in a while."

"Now stop being stubborn and apply it."

If the pillow was a person, I'd have choked the life out of them. The man was right. If I didn't know better, I'd say he had a superpower of his own. What I couldn't decide, was it easing heroes' psychological burdens or aggravating them into submission. The verdict was out for the moment.

"Fine." Yes, I was being a giant man-child. But for three months, he had taken the time to understand me. He wanted to help, and I couldn't deny his ability to cut through my crap and get to the source of my problems. I wouldn't tell him that, but it was true.

"Same time next week?"

"About that…" I set the pillow aside, patting it as if I was asking for forgiveness. "I'm supposed to be at the bridge dedication. Can we move it back a day?"

He reached for his day planner, flipping through the pages. With a snap shut, he nodded. "Thursday it is. Now, go put in the work."

I would have gladly engaged in a verbal duel and explained all the work I had been putting in. If he knew how the number of times I took a deep breath while saving the city, or reminded myself to let go of anger when Alejandro stole my last piece of bacon, he'd have been impressed. Instead, I eyed the door leading out of his office. He glanced over his shoulder and returned with a smile.

"Again?" Dr. Solaris asked.

"Every single time."

With a slight nod, he ended the session. I set the pillow aside and reached the door. With a hiss, the hydraulic locks pulled into the door. If this was how he protected our privacy, it made me wonder if there were other defensive mechanisms hidden behind his diploma or the box of tissues.

"All good?"

Aiden looked up from an issue of Revelations. I stopped, rolling my eyes as he held it up, pointing at the cover. Of course, I knew the journalist behind spotlighting

Vanguard's newest hero. The image of me holding a pose bordered on gaudy, but it had landed him cover billing.

"I hope the reporter captured just how sexy I am."

He snorted. "Or how single you're about to be."

Aiden had insisted I see a therapist. At first I protested, but after seeing me at my best and worst, he was certain which version of me he wanted to date. But that hadn't been the catalyst, even if it was a well-intentioned shove. It was him asking, "Is this who you want to be?"

Like each time before, he wrapped his arms around my neck. Not once had he asked about the sessions or what I talked about with the doctor. No, Aiden knew better. Instead, he took a moment to acknowledge my efforts and check in with me.

With a kiss on the cheek, he held me close. "Everything okay?"

"It's getting there." Emotional honesty, not my strongest trait. But with Aiden, he had seen me at my worst, and yet he still sat in a gray waiting room to ensure I wasn't alone. "I'm doing better."

"I'm proud of you." He whispered the words as he rested his chin on my shoulder.

"Me too." Dr. Solaris made it part of our weekly ritual for me to take time and acknowledge my successes. Our first session had all been about brute strength or imprisoning a bad guy. Now, they were about accepting the parts of myself I didn't particularly like or taking a moment to reflect on my rush to judgment.

They also included being vulnerable. I could stop a mind-control machine from enslaving the people of Vanguard, but indulging in matters of the heart, that remained a source of discomfort.

"Do you want to grab sushi?"

"Can we get it to go?"

"If you don't want—"

But I was getting better.

"Sushi sounds perfect." I kissed him on the cheek. "On the couch, so I can curl up in your lap after and watch T.V."

"My couch or yours?"

───────

There were two gray towels on the rack in the bathroom. I had spent enough nights at Aiden that he had promoted me to having my own towel. I couldn't help but blush. He understood the difficulty of expressing my emotions with words.

The water evaporated from my skin as the fire rolled from head to toe. I didn't need the towel, but the fact he had learned my love language, that was a feat unto itself.

I froze at the thought.

"Love," I whispered. The word had hung on the tip of my tongue more than once as he caressed my chest until I fell asleep. For all we had been through, I hoped he under-stood that word fueled every action.

"Xander," Aiden called from the living room.

Was he in danger? I flung the door open with enough force it pulled from the hinges. I expected to see a villain standing on the fire escape. But all that greeted me was Aiden reclining on the couch in nothing but a jockstrap.

"Uh..." I eyed the door. "I'll fix that."

"Just like the window?" I glanced at the taped cracks on the glass. Okay, I really needed to practice more with my everyday strength. At this rate, somebody was going to catch on by the property damage I left in my wake.

"You can work it off." The devilish smirk spread across his face before he glanced at the bulge barely hidden by the sparse bit of fabric. Suddenly, the broken door didn't seem so important.

I stepped between him and the coffee table. One of the suit's arms pushed the table out of the way, giving me space to kneel between his legs. I appreciated that an alien suit complimented my libido. Even more amazing, Aiden hardly raised an eyebrow when I used my powers for a little extra oomph in the bedroom.

"You are beautiful." The words were breathy and didn't come close to describing the awe before me. I kneeled, running my hand down his chest, tracing the hair as it spread across his stomach. Aiden struggled to comprehend that a guy with a belly and thick legs could be admired. For three months, a day didn't pass where I neglected to remind him.

With each kiss across his stomach, I counted my blessings. It ended with wrapping my hands under his ass and resting my head on the softest part of his torso. As he ran his hand across my scalp, I couldn't imagine a better definition of heaven.

His grip tightened around my neck as he guided me lower. Oh. Scratch that. The tent in his jock might be a better definition. The slight twitch from his cock might prove that he was excited, but the urging as he pushed me down was a first for him taking charge.

With each kiss down his cloth-covered groin, he let a soft moan slip from his lips. He wasn't shy in the bedroom once the clothes came off, but he had never taken charge before. It might be new, but the split second it took me to reach rock-hard status proved that it was a welcome change of pace.

There were no commands as he pulled the fabric aside. He didn't need to say a word. I hadn't said the word, not aloud. But I pushed that statement outward like I did the fire. I could put words into action and show him how much I loved him. Before I could dwell on the thought, I swallowed his cock.

Aiden's hips bucked, burying himself until his belly pressed against my forehead. I was thankful he didn't wield a massive dick as I struggled to breathe. I could have relented at any moment, but I didn't want to pull away until he let me. Just when I approached my limit, Aiden let go, his body relaxing as he panted.

"Damn," he gasped.

I sucked in air and returned to swallowing his cock, running my tongue along the underside with each downward motion. If I thought he'd sit back and let me have my fun, I was sorely mistaken. As he held my head, thrusting in and out of my mouth, he had me nearly gagging before pulling out. In three months, he had been taking notes and learning the language of my body.

I squeezed my cock, excited every time he moaned. I had to pace myself. Apparently, an in-control Aiden pushed all the right buttons.

He growled through clenched teeth. Holding my head in place, I could feel his cock thicken. I gladly buried him toward the back of my throat, swallowing as he came. What he lacked in length, he made up in girth, and even that paled compared to when he finished.

"Damn," he grunted.

I let his cock slip from my mouth before resting my head on his leg. While I stroked myself, I continued licking at his head. I was content making myself come, especially if it meant making Aiden continue with the grunts and moans.

"That was hot," I said between kissing his shaft. Unlike me, Aiden didn't go flaccid once he finished. I had found myself a multi-session champ, which meant I could go all evening teasing and playing.

"Yeah." He shook his head, widening his eyes as if he were waking from a dream. "Come here."

He hooked his hands under my armpits, pulling me until I was half-lying, half-sitting on his body. I never grew tired of feeling this handsome man, *my* handsome man, underneath me.

"Somebody is in a mood," I whispered. He held the side of my head. While I thought I infused my actions with the emotions boiling beneath the surface, it was nothing compared to Aiden. He kissed as if there wasn't another man in the world. When his tongue found its way into my mouth, it was my turn to gasp.

Bits of flame found their way along my arms. I worried they'd burn him until he let out a slight laugh, patting at them until they vanished. "Losing control, huh?"

That bastard. He knew exactly what he did to me. "In more ways than one." It was my turn to grin.

I might have super strength, but even without powers, Aiden was no slouch. He grabbed me by the thighs, sitting me upright in his lap.

"Why the sudden take-charge attitude?"

"Too much?" The worry flashed across his face. I remembered the scared man I dragged into the shower. We had come a long way, but this newfound confidence was still fragile.

I kissed him in an attempt to quiet those lingering insecurities. Leaning my forehead against his, I wrapped my arms around his neck. "Too much would mean there's a world where I could get enough of you."

He rolled his eyes. "Mind control? Possession? I know my Xander isn't this cheesy."

Okay, maybe I laid it on thick. "I was just curious."

"You spend the day making life or death decisions. Why not take one or two off your plate?"

His hands found their way to my hips. They crept around until he held my ass, showing me he was in control. He wiggled his hips, adjusting himself as he lowered me onto his lap. It was my turn to gasp as his cock slid down the crack of my ass.

In three months, our nightly romps ended with me buried inside Aiden. After a long day, I'd come in this sexy man and then reach around and play with his cock until he finished. If I was lucky, we'd fall asleep in that position and resume partway through the night. He had casually grazed my ass while slurping the length of my cock, but changing roles had never come up in our recaps of the previous night.

His eyes begged for permission. I couldn't remember the last time I had let a man top me. I had always been in control, the one making the... Aiden wasn't asking for himself. His eyes weren't asking, they were offering.

Before, if a hookup had dared venture down that

avenue, I'd have politely rejected by flipping them over. I didn't want myself in a position where I relinquished control. I wasn't good at it, but with Aiden, I wanted to try. If every action tonight was to say, "I love you," I'd say yes.

I spit in my hand before reaching back, coating his already slick cock. I leaned back, almost too eager. As the head slid inside, I let out a gasp, my muscles tightening. Being struck down by a Lightning God didn't cause as much of a shock as the sensation of Aiden's girth slipping in.

"You okay?"

I bit my lip as I closed my eyes. I rested a hand on his chest and the moment my fingers touched the hair, my muscles relaxed. While I adjusted, my cock had leaked enough to leave a trail of wet hair on his stomach.

I started a slight rock, gyrating my hips just enough to feel another inch. I moaned loud enough the neighbors were going to need a cigarette. I threw my head back, sliding down the length of his shaft.

"Damn, you're thick."

"You say the sweetest things."

It would only take a couple of strokes and I'd cover Aiden in cum. Even without touching myself, I had to think of anything other than my penis. Math? Sports? The flight time of Pulse, the human rocket?

"Fuck me." Not my more graceful line, but it was accurate. Aiden, the world's sexiest boyfriend, had stepped up to the plate and taken control. It was a gift I offered few men, and from this moment, I'd be relinquishing it to him regularly.

His hands held my thighs in place as he pulled out. With a simple motion, I felt empty, and I wanted him to fill that void. With a thrust, I let out a moan. He repeated the action, drilling into me with determination. But it wasn't until he wrapped his arms around me, pulling me into a bear hug, that I found myself at home.

"Come in me." It was a quiet request, although I wanted to growl it loud enough for the neighbors to partake.

He didn't need encouragement. Pushing as deep as he could manage, Aiden growled into my ear. The sensation of him humming, of his cock thickening—I hadn't been prepared. There was no point in resisting.

"I'm going to come."

He let me go, to lean back with him still buried. He slid a hand under my cock. With a gentle squeeze, the tingling coursed through my body. He moaned again as I tensed, milking the last drop from his body.

The room lit up as the fire raced down the sides of my face, across my shoulders, and along my arms. I would have jumped off him, except his hand held my thigh in place. He leaned away from the fire, but he made no indication he'd let me go. Aiden accepted me and my weird, and as I struggled to catch my breath, I couldn't hold back.

"I love you."

As I waved the fire off, the room remained silent except for our panting. I didn't know the protocol. It was my first time saying those words to another man. I couldn't ignore that I had just covered him in cum and then followed it with an "I love you" chaser. I suddenly felt exposed, even more than having a man buried inside me.

Starting to stand, he held me in place.

"You know it doesn't count while riding my cock." It took a moment before I realized he was giving me grief. To accentuate the sentiment, he flashed a toothy smile.

"Fine." I sat up, forcing his cock from my ass, causing him to grunt at the sensitivity. "I love you."

"I've known," he whispered. He pulled me close. "I love you too." Then he sealed the statement with a kiss.

Now I wanted to spend the night cuddling with him, the man I loved. "Bedtime?"

"Sure." He pointed at his stomach. "Let me go wash this off. Tonight though..." He patted me on the side of the face. "You're the little spoon."

"If I must."

"You must."

It was the first of many...

EPILOGUE 2

"WHY THE HELL DID THEY NOT SEE THE VILLAIN SOONER? And why the heck did he save the day? He spent the entire movie complaining and then turns around and does that?"

I forgot that watching a movie with Griffin was a lesson in patience. It only got worse when he insisted we see the latest superhero film. Why we needed to watch a fictional movie about heroes when they were flying outside our windows, I'll never know.

I stood from the table, collecting the plates from the dinner table. After the movie, Sebastian had been kind enough to let us descend on his apartment, far nicer than anything the three of us had. He also had the best Chinese takeout in the city. The least I could do was be a pleasant guest and help clean up.

"I liked the suits," Sebastian chimed.

"They looked comfortable," I added. "Spandex is probably more breathable than leather."

Aiden shot me a look. While having a secret identity meant frequently lying to those around me, I had given him full access to my alter ego. But the rest of the breakfast club remained in the dark. It was the only way I could keep them safe from the growing number of villains that'd see Lionheart dead.

"How are things going at the Beacon?" Aiden asked. I found it amusing that Griffin worked at his boyfriend's rival company. I imagined there were dozens of arguments about which magazine was crushing it.

"Did you see the new issue?" Sebastian jumped in, heading to the living room to dig through the magazines on the coffee table. "The cover alone…"

"You're going to make me blush." Griffin tried to sound modest, but he couldn't hide the pride in his voice. Good for him. After everything he went through with both magazines, life had turned around. Dr. Solaris' voice echoed in the back of my head.

"Griffin," I started. God, why was it hard to toss out a casual compliment without sounding like a squishy mess? "I have to say, you've been doing pretty damned well for yourself. I've never seen you this confident in your work." See, Doc, I can highlight the good things too.

"That's…" Griffin spun about in his chair, eyeing me. "Almost sweet? What have you done to Xander?"

I ignored the jab. Instead, I set the plates in the sink and wandered around Sebastian's apartment. It was obvious he made good money at the magazine. The man had impeccable taste, the dark reds and blacks woven through every piece of artwork on the walls and even the throw pillows on the couch. I should have expected as much. Griffin had said the man was an amazing artist.

The open concept floor plan made it easy to move from the dining room to the kitchen and into the living room. While I inspected the art, Griffin and Aiden moved to the couch, returning to their discussion about the movie. It was ironic, Aiden dating a superhero and Griffin in love with the entire genre. If only Griffin knew...

"Xander," Sebastian started washing the dishes. "Mind drying?"

This double date had been Aiden's idea. He wanted to meet my friends, and truth be told, I wanted them to meet the man who saved me from myself. I hadn't expected him and Griffin to hit it off so well. Sebastian, however, had been tougher to crack. He was far more reserved, and other than working at the magazine, I knew nothing about him. For Aiden's sake, I'd keep trying.

"Sure, might as well let them geek out."

"Once Griffin gets started on superheroes, he'll ramble until he tuckers himself out."

I laughed. "Do you know how many times at breakfast

he's gone on about a superhero? Then we find out it's not a real person but a character in a comic book."

Sebastian stopped scrubbing to laugh. "I know exactly what you mean."

He handed me a dripping plate, and I snatched a rag off the counter. Okay, small talk that didn't include mentioning bodily fluids in the ambulance. How hard could this be?

"I like your art." Wow, Xander. When this was over, I'd be sure to Google how to make small talk.

"Thanks. Griffin mentioned you work as a medic. How's that going?"

"Now that heroes are powered again, it's back to normal. I didn't think I'd miss saving people who could rip open portals in space. It's a very different type of medicine, but I'm glad to be of service."

Since I uttered the phrase, "Maybe heroes aren't so bad," at breakfast, Griffin had made it his mission to open my eyes to the secret lives of heroes. Apparently, working at the magazine gave him a special insight. While I bit my tongue, holding back snide comments, he did, in fact, give me useful information. Who knew there was an etiquette about fighting another hero's arch-nemesis?

"What about your other job?"

I froze as he handed me another plate. Right now, the only people who knew my secret were Aiden, Hellcat, Lei, and William. Had I slipped up? Did William finally wake up from his coma and tell the prison guards? This had been a worry in the back of my head ever since the hero community watched me rescue Aiden. Had somebody spilled the beans?

"No side hustles for me." It was as convincing as I could make the statement.

I glanced from the burly hand holding the plate to his eyes. If he hadn't been holding the dish, I'd have dropped it on the floor. His iris' vanished, replaced by a brilliant white light. They returned to normal quickly, and I'd have worried I imagined the glimpse of power, except the smirk remained on his lips. Sebastian and I had more in common than I originally believed.

"I want to talk to you about joining the Night Guard."

—THE END—

Follow Alejandro's Story in
Men of Vanguard Book 3:
Iridescent Light

Want More Men of Vanguard?
Join Ryder's Scandalous Super's Newsletter

AFTERWORD

I am a gay man obsessed with superheroes. As a kid, I had no role models, and that hasn't changed much as an adult. Because of this, I bringing my relationships, sex life, and love of comics to the forefront in the *Men of Vanguard Series*. The characters in these books reflect personal experiences and themes set against a fictional backdrop.

ABOUT THE AUTHOR

Superheroes stories are at core of Ryder O'Malley's origin story. Refusing to read as a child, everything changed with the first stack of comics. He has always been a fan of forbidden romances within the pages of comics. It should be expected that he'd turn around and start writing his own stories filled with sexy, super, man-on-man action. Ryder's novels draw on his own experiences as a gay man in search of love.

Ryder lives in Boston, Massachusetts and will soon be making the trek to Glasgow, Scotland to join his long-time partner and live his happily-ever-after. When he's not writing, he can be found working on client book covers (which means he's admiring the abs of muscular men with a little bit of chest hair.)

Ingram Content Group UK Ltd.
Milton Keynes UK
UKHW041837180523
421997UK00011B/155/J